I am Always Here With You

Himanshu Rai

I am Always Here With You

HIMANSHU RAI

Srishti
PUBLISHERS & DISTRIBUTORS

SRISHTI PUBLISHERS & DISTRIBUTORS
Registered Office: N-16, C.R. Park
New Delhi – 110 019
Corporate Office: 212A, Peacock Lane
Shahpur Jat, New Delhi – 110 049
editorial@srishtipublishers.com

First published by
Srishti Publishers & Distributors in 2019

Printed at Repro Knowledgecast Limited, Thane

We live once, and in one life,
we breathe a million times.
I want you both to smile
more than our breaths.
I am always here with you,
Sona & Rhythm.

Today, I cannot smile at you. But will smile remembering all the laughs we shared.

Love you, Papa.

Marriages are made in heaven. This is what we keep hearing. Marriage isn't just a ring worn on a finger, or a signed piece of paper. It is not something endured, but something sweetly savoured. It is the union of two hearts beating as one, each that would sacrifice for the other's happiness and well-being. It's a union of two souls which will smile and cry together. It's a union of two bodies which will live for each other, forever in love and care.

I was standing with Ashima, my wife, in our bedroom. She was all set to leave for the banquet hall, holding a bouquet of red roses in her hand. She was dressed in a red lehenga with golden work and a dupatta over her head. She was looking as beautiful as ever. Her hands adorned with red and gold bangles were creating a magical effect on her soft white hands.

I loved her lips and complimented her. Today when they are glowing with wine coloured lipstick, I could not take my eyes away from them. Ashima sat in front of the dressing mirror. Standing behind her, I looked at her with a smile on my face.

Her deep thinking eyes were looking gorgeous with perfectly lined eyeliner. With the fine make-up and hair-do, she looked ravishing.

The sound of guests laughing and chatting outside our room was not distracting me that day. I was lost in her beauty which I'd miss forever in a few hours. But I am happy today.

"Kartik, I am sorry for leaving you today. You know that I will miss you forever. I know you are hoping that I'd stay, but it's just impossible. We started our love story when we were children, and today, I need to move on, and that too for your love. You were always with me when I needed you, and today, when I am taking a new path in my life, I will not say that I will miss you, because we only miss someone whom we forget. You are a part of my soul, my breath, and my life and I will always love you, until my last breath."

I could feel her pain. I could see tears rolling down her cheeks, but that day I could not stop her from crying, because I was happy. It was her wedding day. She kept looking at the mirror, while I stood behind her, watching her.

I wanted to shout, but no one wanted to hear my voice. I wanted to come back, but it was too late. I wanted to hug her again, but she was no longer mine. Because it was her wedding day – my wife's wedding.

She stood holding her lehenga and turned towards me. She looked beautiful as never before and I wanted to hold her and never let her go. But instead, I took two steps back and went to the balcony to let my soul cry.

1

Three years ago

It was six in the morning, and I was still sleeping, lost in my dreams, when the alarm clock started ringing. Without opening my eyes, I moved my hand to turn it off and pulled the blanket to cover my face. Winters in Delhi are chilly, and waking up early has always been tough for me. I tried to move my left hand to the side and hug Ashima. But she was not there. I could hear her in the washroom. Laziness kept me buried in bed, and as I moved my hand back, I felt something cold. The mattress on my side was wet. I immediately woke up and stood up to call out to her, "Ashima! Ashima! What is this? Why is the bed wet?"

Within no time, Ashima opened the door of the washroom with her charming smile.

"What happened, janu? It's just the glass of water that slipped from my hand," she replied, smiling and fresh. I placed my hand on my face and buried myself in bed again. She usually looked stunning in the morning, but that day, she looked different. She had tied up her hair and had oiled it. She seemed quite busy. The warm lights in our green bedroom always made her seem out of the world.

"She walked over to my side of the bed with her dazzling smile, and ran her soft hands over my forehead, kissing it softly. She then turned to move away, but I took hold of her hand, pulling her towards me. I always loved her in that red t-shirt. "Stop, Kartik! I need to do something urgently. Get up and get ready for office."

Disheartened, I let her go towards the kitchen. I did call out to her, "I love you, Angel." Yes, I used to call her Angel since we were in class tenth.

"I love you too, Teddy," she replied from the kitchen, her nickname for me since our school days. But let me be clear, I am not at all like a teddy bear. I am six feet in height with a perfect physique and am clean-shaven.

I was always crazy about her smile. I had first met her at our school in Dehradun when we were in our tenth class. It was my first day at school, and when I saw her smiling, she won over my heart. It was love at sight for me, but not for her. She took seven long years to say yes.

I removed the blanket and tried to step down from the bed, but the floor was a total mess. A bottle of moisturizer, a tube of cream, a comb, and my shaving cream – everything was on the floor. I was confused about how all that stuff came to be there. I've known Ashima for the last nine years, and she is a neat person. How were the things lying on the floor? Was she angry with me? But she never did this, even when she was mad at me. First I thought I'd ask her, but then changed my mind and picked up all the stuff and put it back.

In no time I was back in the bedroom, dressing up for office. I could hear her singing in a low voice.

"Abhi na jao chhod kar, ki dil abhi bhara nahi.."

I smiled as I listened to her and went towards her with slow steps. She was facing the kitchen platform. I held her from the back with my hands on her waist. I loved her in her pyjamas and top she wore to bed at night. She smiled and stopped singing. I kissed her softly on her left cheek. She smiled and replied, "What happened, Teddy? You don't wanna go to office today?"

"You said, *abhi na jao chhodkar, ki dil abhi bhara nahi.* So I thought let me help you with it," I replied, being naughty.

"Don't try to act oversmart," she replied turning towards me, with a spoon in her hand. I was 6 feet tall, and she was 5 feet and an inch, so when she stood close to me, she usually got buried in my chest. I kissed her on her head.

"Your breakfast is on the dining table. Go and have it, fast! If you get late, you will get stuck in a jam," Ashima replied pushing me out of the kitchen. I took a seat at the table. She put a bowl of something in front of me.

"What is this, Ashima? It tastes like milk," I asked her, as it was something different. It was sweet and smelled good. I took another spoon of it when Ashima came out of the kitchen and stood at the door, smiling at me.

"What? Why are you smiling? Tell me what is this?"

She kept smiling, sat down next to me and then asked, "Who can get your bed wet? Who will make your room messy? Who will eat this milky dish?"

She again started smiling.

Hearing her, I stopped eating, and my mind started running at gigahertz speed. I put my spoon back into the bowl and took two to three spoons full, one after the other, and then replied anxiously, jumping from my seat, "This is baby food! Yes... this is baby food. A baby will wet my bed; a baby will make my room messy. You are pregnant?! I am going to be a father. Am I correct Ashima, answer me?"

I shouted in happiness and stood up from my chair to hug her. Ashima was smiling with tears of joy in her eyes. She nodded softly, and I hugged her back. I took her in my arms and leaned my face down towards her to kiss her. She kissed me back. I was really excited, but she looked calm.

She let me sit back on the chair, and she stood in front of me, smiling and ran her fingers through my hair. "You know Kartik, I came to know yesterday, and since then, I've been wondering how to surprise you. This is one of the most significant gifts god has given to both of us. Our nine years of love will be in front of us in the form of a baby. I am feeling complete today, and it's all because of you. I love you, and would only like to ask you something."

I nodded, and she continued, "When the baby will keep you up the whole night, will you still love me the same way? I may not walk as fast, will you slow down for me? Will you mind driving your car slowly for the next nine months? I'll not get time for myself and may look ugly and untidy. Will you still love me? I may not get time to cook for you. Will you still love me the same? Our home will be a mess, and you might get disturbed by the crying, but will you still love me the same way? I'll be vomiting for the next three months, will you still be by my side?"

Before she could ask me further questions. I placed my finger on her lips and made her sit. I went down on my knees and put my head on her lap, like a baby and replied, "I know this lap will be booked after a few months, but I'll be the one enjoying it the most. I know you'll vomit, and I need to help you out, but I would be the one cherishing it the most. I know he or she will keep me awake, and I need to make him or her sleep in my arms, but I would be the one enjoying it the most, seeing the tiny smiles in his dreams. I know the baby will be your priority, but I'll be the one enjoying my love growing. I started liking you when you were a kid, I loved you when you got older, and will love you until my last breath."

I completed my answer and went silent. She placed her head on mine, and we both smiled. Being in love was not only about us. It's a story from 'us' to 'we', and the day you feel the smile on every 'we', your life is a success. We both understood this concept of life and agreed to become 'we'.

"Can you come early today? We can meet my gynocologist, Dr Sangeeta in Apollo hospital," Ashima questioned.

I stood up and replied adjusting my shirt, "Definitely Angel, I will. You please take care now."

I took my laptop and started moving towards the door, when she asked softly, "Kartik, please do not tell our parents and relatives yet. Let's be assured first."

She knew I was thrilled, and it would be tough for me to keep the news to myself, but I smiled and assured her, "I will not be telling anyone, *pakka.*"

She waved to me. I kissed her again and left.

2

We lived on the first floor in a rented flat in Noida. And as I stepped down, I could feel the cold breeze of January. It was cloudy, with no sign of the sun. I could hardly see my cab which was standing at some distance due to the fog, but I finally managed to spot it, as the headlights were on. I started walking towards it when I heard Ashima from the balcony, "Teddy, wait!"

I looked up to check and she threw a muffler towards me, "*Thand bahut hai,* take care." I caught the muffler and then replied, "Go inside immediately and wear some warm clothes."

She smiled and said bye. It was her old habit – she loved winters. She would be eating ice cream; she would be wearing short dresses and no warm clothes. Her funda regarding the weather was, "*Life mein weather enjoy nahi kiya to kya kiya.* God has given us the weather to enjoy." But now I needed to be strict with her as she had a little one to take care of.

I reached the cab with my laptop on my side and opened the door. My office was in Gurgaon, and it would take me around an hour-and-a-half to reach. I was working with a marketing firm, but preferred residing in Noida as Ashima's parents were in Greater Noida. It was easier for us to visit them. As my pick up was the first, I usually took a nap on my way to office. But that day, I was too excited. I placed my laptop on the side and put my head back, closed my eyes and starting recollecting the days of our school when I had first met Ashima. Within no time, nostalgia took me back in time.

Back in 2007

"Don't be disheartened, beta! Feel fresh and enthusiastic; it's your first day in school," my mother said, cheering me up. My father had left his MTNL job in Delhi and joined Idea cellular company as the Head of Operations in Dehradun. I was not at all happy leaving my Delhi school and friends in my tenth class. But Papa suggested that shifting and adjusting was still comfortable in the tenth as I needed to start preparing for my entrance exams after this. I was the only son, but my father never let me think like that. He was my friend, but strict when it was required. My mummy was a housewife and lovely by nature. She loved chatting with everyone she found interesting, and if not, she could build an interest in them. My father, on the other hand, spoke less and always to the point; he always took time to gel with others.

I was a pampered child, but not a spoiled one. I was good in studies and extra curriculars. I loved swimming and singing and my ambition in life was to trek and swim. My father knew my weakness, and so he agreed to send me to Doon Global Boarding School. He told me that I could be an international swimming champion by practicing in school. And as Dehradun was closer to Mussoorie, I could go trekking whenever I wanted. Although, I was not a small kid, nevertheless I was excited about trekking in the hills.

"Ya, Mummy, I am excited, but missing my Delhi school," I replied picking up my bag. I was a day scholar, which meant I'd not be staying in the school hostel.

"Come, let me drop you to school," Papa said picking up his car keys.

"No, it's okay Papa, I will take my cycle." I always loved cycling, and as we lived in Chakrata, which was near the school, I wanted to bike to school along the road between the lush green valley.

"As you wish, but go slowly, it's a new place."

"Sure Papa," I assured him and picked up my cycle keys.

With a small bag on my back, I started riding my sports bike on the plain, open and traffic free road of Chakrata. The beauty of the tall green trees on both sides of the road was mesmerising. I had never seen such a pleasant view in Delhi. The soft cold breeze was hitting my face, and I wanted to keep cycling until the road ended. The atmosphere had a pleasant fragrance of the vegetation all around. I breathed in deeply as I reached school.

I parked my cycle at the cycle stand and went in to look for my class. The school was beautiful, with a vast campus. My Delhi school was in one big building and had just a small playground. As I walked on the lane made up of stones, I observed students running towards a particular area. Since I had joined after one month of the session had already passed, the other students were more familiar with the rules and regulations. I became worried. I was wondering where to go. And then I saw a man asking students to rush, maybe for the assembly. I went up to him.

"Dear, please move fast for assembly. It's starting now," he said looking at me.

"Sorry, sir. I am a new student. I don't know where to go. Help me, please," I replied in a soft tone to him, with my hands folded at the back.

"Which class?"

"Sir, tenth," I replied

He took a pause, and then replied, "You come with me. After assembly, you may meet the Principal. She will give you all the details."

I nodded and started following him. He was a middle-aged man, bald, dark and looked very strict. He started walking and I followed him. After crossing the first row of classrooms, we reached a significant open ground where all the students were standing, in all probability according to their class sections.

"Remain silent and stand at the corner," the man asked me to stand at the back of all the students, under the corridor shed. Some teachers were standing there and looked at me with exploring eyes. I was afraid, tensed, and lonely. I started missing my old school even more.

Dressed in a pale yellow shirt, brown trousers, and a black tie, I stood with my eyes down. I was feeling nostalgic and annoyed, remembering my old friends when I heard the prayer on the loudspeakers.

"My Father in heaven, Holy be your name, your kingdom come..."

That soft, polite and sweet voice made me look up.

My eyes passed hundreds of students standing in an array to the small stage in front, on which a few students were conducting assembly. And a beautiful girl, wearing a pale yellow shirt, brown skirt till her knees with her hair pinned into a ponytail, with her joined hands and closed eyes was reciting the prayer. I wanted to concentrate on praying, but my eyes would not agree to blink, nor would my head agree to bend. It was the first time I was feeling something different for someone. She was my Ashima. Just by looking at her, my nostalgic feeling evaporated and my heart condensed in her smile. As she finished, I realized I had a strange smile on my face.

There was pin-drop silence during assembly, but I was out of the world. My mind was running very fast, creating stories, questions and answering them all on my own. I was admiring everything about her – from the way the breeze blew her hair to the lilt of her voice. To me, she looked like water in the heat of the desert. But what made me fall head over heels for her was the way she smiled and blinked her eyes. The way she bent her head, the way she adjusted her braids, the way she was calm, and the way she looked naughty. Everything about her was driving me towards her. I knew it was a crush, but, kya kahun doston, *that crush was something I was in love with. I continued observing her, as she took her position back with the other students on the stage.*

Soon, the assembly got over. Sir showed me the principal's cabin and asked me to wait till he got the details of my class.

He seemed like quite a supportive teacher. He went inside after taking my details.

The principal's office was huge, with the school emblem on the door, and the list of toppers from various years on the right side. By then, I was losing connect with the girl whom I had just seen during assembly, and was reading the names of the students on the notice board. Few junior girls and boys where decorating the large notice board placed outside the principal's cabin. I was trying to read the content on the notice board when sir came out of the room and called me, "Kartik, please come here."

Hearing him, I rushed towards him. "Yes sir."

"Your class is X, section D. It's on the other side of this building. Let me take you there. By the way, I am a mathematics teacher, and my name is Sir Patel."

"Thanks a lot, sir, for all your help." And we started walking, while he asked me, "You are new to Dehradun or have you just changed your school?"

"Sir, I am from Delhi. My father got transferred here."

"Where does he work?" he asked me another question, but before I could reply, he called someone with a loud voice, "Ashima, please come here."

I turned to my left, and to my surprise, she was the same girl whom I had been admiring. She took long steps and came fast, although she was carrying a stack of copies, all covered and labelled in her hands.

"Yes sir, you called me?" she asked coming close to us, and again her voice brought a smile to my face. The dimple on her left cheek was perfect.

"He is Kartik – a new student in our school. He is in your section. Please take him to your class and introduce him to

Mrs Vandana, your class teacher," Patel sir told her and left, his hands in his pockets.

"Hi! I am Ashima. Welcome to our school," she told me with a beautiful smile on her face. She was fair, with pink lips and cheeks.

"Hi! I am Kartik, may I help you?" I asked and took half the copies as we started walking down the corridor towards the class.

After walking for a few steps, I tried to start a conversation. "It was a long prayer. You said it very nicely."

"I've been in this school since nursery and have been reciting since then," she replied smiling.

Her voice was melodious, crushed in her soft breath and mixed with a smile.

"Oh, I thought…." I stopped in the middle, as she showed me our class, pointing her finger. Just as she stepped in front of me, I said, "I heard prayers are for angels, but your voice was sounding like an angel's, reciting the prayer."

I suddenly stopped walking as she stopped hearing my words. Still not facing me, her hair at the side of her ears were moving in the breeze. She turned and replied with a naughty smile, "And you are looking like a teddy bear, with the bag on your back and copies in your hands." Her smiled relaxed me, as she entered the class.

She introduced me to Mrs Vandana, our English and class teacher. She welcomed me and introduced me to all the students. That was my first interaction with my Ashima. My smiling, energetic, lively, beautiful Ashima.

"Sir, please wake up, we have reached your office in Gurgaon," my cab driver woke me up. I realized I had been dreaming of the best time of my life, but now I needed to get to work.

Someone said '*Life isn't about finding yourself. Life is about creating yourself.*' But when you reach far creating your life, you realize finding life was much better; at least your family and friends were with you.

I stepped in front of the DLF building in Cyber City, Gurugram, and walked among thousands, with my laptop on my shoulder and dreams in my eyes. Every day when I walked to my office, I felt like the balloon seller who used to come to our lane when we were small kids. He carried a bunch of balloons tied to a wooden ply like thing. Same as me and the others. Now, our laptop bags replaced the wooden stick, but we were the same – running and moving around every day, to earn money.

I took my seat, opened my laptop. While waiting for it to boot, I dialled Ashima's number.

"Father in Heaven. Holy be your name…" I just started as she picked up the call, but got stuck after one line intentionally to let her continue. And she did, "Your kingdom come, you will be done, as it is in heaven…."

"What happened Teddy? *Is prayer ki yaad kahan se aa gayi aaj subah subah?*"

I took a pause, relaxed in my seat, smiled and then replied, "Today I got the news that our love is coming to this world," paused and then continued, "So madam, how can I forget the first word which I had heard from the lips of the love of my life."

I could sense her blushing in her silence. She finally said lovingly, "You still remember everything?"

"Yaad to use rakhte hain, jise bhulte hain… tumhari har baat to hum kabhi bhulte hi nahi." And we both laughed. She said, "I love you" and asked me to get back to work.

I don't know who invented these three magical words, but whoever did, must have been in love with fairies, as they are the ones spreading love in the universe.

I placed my mobile on my desk, typed my login ID and password in the laptop, but then stopped, thought for a while and then picked up my mobile to sent a message to my Ashima:

Since the day I have seen you, my lips have parted wider, smiling. I smiled hearing your voice, I smiled meeting you, I smiled walking with you, I smiled talking to you, and today, I am again smiling, hearing that we are going to be three now! Angel, I love you.

3

"It's the first trimester, Ashima. Congrats!" Dr Sangeeta continued looking at the reports. "You are pregnant, and you need to take care of yourself now, and the same goes for you also, Kartik." She looked at me, and I could only nod, being nervous and excited. She tried to explain to us in detail what changes Ashima was about to experience in herself. "You will experience a lot of symptoms during your first trimester as your body will adjust to the hormonal changes. In the early days, it will not be showing much on the outside of the body, but inside, many changes will be taking place."

I was listening very carefully as we both lived alone, and I needed to take care of her during this period.

"You may have nausea and vomiting, which a woman typically feels during her first month of pregnancy. You may feel tired, and your digestion system may not work properly for a few days, causing a decreased interest in eating. Apart from these, you may experience emotional swings, which may range from weepiness and forgetfulness to fear, anxiety and excitement. And for that, Kartik, you need to handle her and keep her happy all the time."

I nodded again and showed my comfort with the idea. I could read feel the anxiety on Ashima's face, but I knew her very well and knew how to get her to overcome that feeling.

The doctor prescribed a few medicines and exercises before we left the hospital. As we started driving back home, Ashima placed her hand softly mine, which was on the gear.

"Kartik, are you not worried?" She looked at me, brooding.

And looking at her I replied, "Let me explain to you in detail, but not here. Let's drive to the Greater Noida Expressway."

She looked confused. Greater Noida Expressway is an eight-lane expressway connecting Noida, and Greater Noida, covered with lush green plants and trees on both sides. The often empty highway exudes a romantic feeling. I knew she loved nature and I wanted to provide her with the most romantic atmosphere at that moment. I turned my car towards the highway. On the way, she kept asking me what I was doing, but I kept smiling and asked her to wait for the surprise.

Within no time, we reached a point which had maximum greenery all around, and was quite for from traffic. I parked my car on the side and asked her to step out. I rushed to the other side to open her door. I took her hand and helped her to step out of the car. She smiled, and I replied, "Welcome to the stars, miss."

"And now, what are we going to do here?" she asked me with a beautiful smile. I took her hand and helped her to sit on the bonnet of the car.

"Are you mad or what, Teddy?"

I could see her smile. This is what I wanted – just a smile on her face. Once she sat there, I lay back on the windshield, propped up on my forearm.

"Hey Angel, put your head on my shoulder," I said.

"Are you mad Kartik? The passing cars will notice us."

"So what, I am enjoying the weather with my wife. Who cares about the passing cars? And do you not want the answer to your question?" I replied with a beatific smile on my face. This made her comfortable.

It was almost nine in the night; the sky was dark. The stars lit up the sky like snow-flakes, yet frozen still, like in an old photograph. Ashima was smiling, feeling the soft wind blowing her hair.

"You asked me if I am worried. But you know this is not the first time this is happening to me." Before Ashima threw a question, I continued softly moving my fingers in her hair, "You know, I read today on Google, that during the first trimester, the heart and lungs begin to develop, and the arms, legs, brain, spinal cord and nerves begin to form."

"My first trimester started when I met you nine years back. I never told you what hormonal changes I felt after meeting you for the first time in school, but today, when Dr Sangeeta was talking to us, I felt that everything had happened the same way to me when I had first met you."

I could feel Ashima's hand on my chest, and it patted me to continue. I softly kissed her on her forehead and proceeded to tell her about the day I had met her for the first time nine years ago.

I remember, when I returned from school after the first day, I could only remember you. I remembered your smile; I remembered your dimples; I remembered your moves.

I finished my dinner and rushed to the terrace to watch the night sky, which I always missed in Delhi. But that day, the night sky was going to be different for me. I climbed up on the overhead water tank on my terrace and lay down on it.

The sky was filled with stars playing hide and seek between the gray clouds. I wanted to count them, but my mind was on a different tangent. I don't know why, but my mind was humming 'Pehla nasha pehla khumaar'. My eyes were looking at the stars, but only saw you in them. Soon I realized that my heart had started beating faster; I was breathing heavily. For me, that night was different. I could feel the effects of love at first sight, which I had never felt before. My hormones were changing my moods.

Again and again, I recalled the morning interaction with you, and all I wanted was to be with you. I was nervous, but happy. I was excited, but fearful. I wanted that night to get over soon so that I could meet you again the next morning. I kept looking at the night sky searching for you, but now I realized I was searching for myself, for you.

I took a pause and looked into her eyes to continue.

Next morning, I was ready for school before time. I wanted to reach earlier so that I could find out where you live and how you come to school. I had my breakfast and cycled fast, so I could reach the school gates before even a single student reached.

It was a different feeling; I didn't know why and what was making me do so, but my mind was not listening to my heart. Everything within me changed.

I could see Ashima smiling at my words, and I continued to narrate my story to her.

I parked my cycle outside the main gate and remained standing there, observing every student who was entering. Some came in the school bus, some in their cars and some on their cycles, but I was worried as I could not see you anywhere. I did not want to miss your entry to school in that rush. I knew if I could find the way by which you come to school, I could also find your address. And that motivation kept me rooted to my position. Finally, I saw you on your pink ladybird cycle.

I turned my face away so that you wouldn't see me, but I was happy. You came to school on your cycle – that meant you lived nearby. Suddenly, my mind started making plans to grab your attention.

You know that day when we entered our classroom after assembly, my heart was telling me to sit next to you or behind you, but my mind, my fearful mind took me to the back seat. One after another, the classes were getting over, but I was busy thinking about how to talk to you and how to get your attention. I was so attentive in observing you, that I remember you were wearing a pink hairband.

"Really, you remember that?" Ashima interrupted, but I smiled and continued.

The whole day, I kept smiling because you were laughing. You entered my life suddenly, and everything changed in one night. You didn't notice, but I adjusted my hair many times that day.

I was not sure what was making me do all that, but after school, I followed you. You were with Seema, and I cycled behind you. I wanted to know your address. I wanted to know everything about you. You were chatting, laughing, talking with Seema, but I was smiling, watching you from behind. And when you entered the railway colony society, I was happy to know you lived so close by.

Every evening since then, I used to cycle from my home to your society, just in case I could find you or at least get a glimpse of you, but in vain. And then, one evening, I was cycling outside your society as usual. Every time I crossed your society gate, I moved my head up to look for you, but found you nowhere, and during my third try, a car from behind hit me. I ended up with a fractured hand and bruises all over.

Ashima pulled herself a little away in astonishment and questioned, "Oh my god, and you are telling me this today? You met with that accident because of this reason?"

I nodded politely.

It was the second day when my mummy came to my room and asked me to go to the drawing room as some of my friends had come to see me. I was not sure who they could be, as I hardly knew anyone. My father had dropped a message in school that I met with an accident and would not be able to attend school for a few days. I was interested in meeting them, perhaps I could make new friends this way. I adjusted my plastered hand and walked to the drawing room, but stopped at the door, finding you sitting there with Seema.

I was nervous, shy and could not understand what to say or do. I never expected you to come. My mummy was asking me to come out, but I was feeling shy. This was the first time any of my female classmates had visited my home, and that too you, my first crush.

It was a different feeling, which I had never had before. I loved that feeling, but nervousness was overtaking my mind. My heart was telling me to smile, but the mind was making me conscious of my body language. I could still feel shivers remembering how my mummy was looking at you.

I stopped and kissed Ashima's forehead.

"Then what?" she asked me softly.

"Then you know what happened. But is this an answer to your question whether I am worried?" I asked. "I was worried that day, feeling that something new was coming in my life, just as you are worried today. I felt multiple changes in me after meeting you, but smiled, considering those changes would bring a smile to the face later too. I was ready to face any challenge in life when I saw you. I no more felt the pain of the fracture and was prepared to drive my cycle back outside your colony within a month because I loved you."

She smiled, and that's all that mattered. "Today, I am facing the same change in me, and yes, you are experiencing the same in your body. But I assure you, this change is for good. If we smile today, we three will smile in the future. I could get you in my life because I accepted those changes. And we will get our baby into this world by accepting changes. Because change is something which can bring a smile and tears as well, but it's we who decide what we want and how we want to see it."

Ashima, with a radiant smile, hugged me, "I love you, my Teddy."

"I have been with you since we were children and I will be with you when our children have their children, because your Teddy loves you a lot."

I then got off the car bonnet and opened the car dash to bring out something wrapped in red gift paper.

"What is this? A gift for me?" she shouted with a big smile on her face. I handed it over to her, and she immediately started unwrapping it, with questions back to back.

"What is in this?"

"You bought this for me?"

"I love you a lot, Teddy."

"Wow, this is so cute," Ashima smiled at the book *Mom & Baby*. She could not wait to hug me.

"This book will help you know what's going on in your body every week, and what care you must take for our baby," I replied, still hugging her.

That day, while driving back, we both discussed the changes we would be facing, and the how we'd as a team handle our baby. Who will be making him or her sleep? Who will wash his or her clothes? Who will clean his or her potty? These were the things we talked about all the way back home.

4

I have known Ashima since our school days, and now when we were going to have our baby, it was making me nostalgic. I still see her as a cute, naughty classmate and friend. Now when she was carrying my baby, I was falling in love with her all the more.

It was eleven in the night, and Ashima was already asleep. But I was still thinking about her and our baby. Dr Sangeeta had informed us that she was six weeks pregnant. I wanted to know all about the six weeks baby growth pattern and the changes my Angel would be facing. So I got up from the bed and picked up the book which I had gifted her. On tiptoe, I went to the other room and switched on the lights to read the chapter about six-week pregnancy.

It said, by the time you know for sure you're pregnant, you might already be five or six weeks pregnant! As per the book, a lot must be happening during this first three months in her body. Formation of cells and implants in the wall of her womb where the baby will be growing. It said the baby grew faster in this trimester, as compared to any other time in the complete cycle. This is the time when a baby's heartbeat can be heard.

I was puzzled reading that, wondering so much was going on in the body of my love. I don't know why, but everything that was happening, I could relate to our past life. The first trimester was similar to my first year with Ashima. A lot of love, confusion, changes and efforts to build a new relationship.

I placed the book on my chest and leaned back to close my eyes, thinking about our school days. I remembered the day we became friends for life.

I was sitting alone in the school library that day, trying to solve some mathematical problems, when Ashima interrupted me with her smile, taking a front seat. She whispered, "Hey, how is your hand, Kartik?"

I looked up with a smile to reply, "Now better, perfectly fine."

I looked at her; she was holding a history book in her hand. She leaned towards me to speak softly, "Why do you always remain alone in school?"

I was happy that she was talking to me and I wanted to have a conversation with her. I leaned towards her to reply, "Shall we talk outside? Someone will scold us here."

She nodded with a smile, and we closed our books. We started walking down the corridor.Once we were outside, a bed of sunflowers blooming in the soft sunlight from the hills lined the path we took. I was silently walking by her side; my heart was beating fast, and then she again questioned, "Are we out here for a walk?"

"Oh! No actually, you know, I am new to the school. Most of the students already have their groups. I am finding it tough to join them."

Ashima heard me and with a pause, took one long step and came in front of me, her ponytail shaking from right to left.

"I am Ashima, will you be my friend?" she presented her hand to me with a dimpled smile. I smiled too. It was a dream come true for me. I extended my hand to shake hers. It was soft, almost like cream. I wanted to keep holding her hand. But in the same instance, I decided that I'd not touch anything with that hand at least for a day. I wanted to keep her touch with me, for as long as possible.

"Thanks a lot for this and also thanks for coming home to show your concern," I replied as we started walking.

"It's perfectly fine, Kartik. Friends must take care of each other. Now if something happens to me, I am sure you'd also come. Will you?" she questioned smiling.

"May god never bring such a day, when I need to visit you after such an incident. Whenever I visit you, I must visit for a smile exchange."

She suddenly stopped, closed her eyes and then flashed her two fingers to me, asking, "Now pick one."

"What is this for?" I questioned.

"Pick one, Kartik," she insisted. I looked at them and then touched her index finger. She then took a deep breath with a relaxed smile.

"It's perfect," she replied with a sly smile.

"*Tell me what it was for?*" I asked again.

She paused and then replied, "*Okay, let me tell you. The index finger was for whenever we meet, we will exchange smiles, and the middle finger was for tears. You picked the index finger, which means we will always meet with a smile.*"

Her explanation showed how much she believed in it, but for me, it was just a game. "*Do you believe in it, or just for fun?*"

"*OMG, you don't believe in it? It works, Mr Kartik, it works,*" she replied slack-jawed. With a naughty smile, I presented my two fingers in front of her and asked her to pick one.

"*You wanna check this out?*" she questioned laughing, while her eyes were moving fast between both the fingers and before I could reply, she picked the index finger.

"*Tell me what it was for and the result?*" she again questioned.

"*Okay, it was for whether you will allow me to go back home cycling along with you.*"

"*And the result?*"

"*That I will tell you in the afternoon when school gets over,*" I confirmed, and she softly pushed me with her shoulder replying, "*You are such a cheat.*"

We walked towards the classroom, chatting about our families and Dehradun. As we entered the class, she was about to go to her desk, when I told her, "*I will be waiting for you outside the main gate after school. Will go back together.*"

I took my seat for the next class, but my heart was excited being her friend.

As our last class got over, I rushed to the washroom to check my hair. I washed my face to look fresh and then picked up my cycle to reach the main gate. My eyes were waiting for Ashima.

I knew she would come, and then we'd be going together, having a lot of fun.

I remained standing, and then she came along with Seema, but without acknowledging me, moved ahead. I kept looking at her, but she ignored me. I realized I was correct – this finger game didn't work, because if it worked, we'd have been cycling together.

I started cycling, but I remained behind her. I kept watching her to understand the reason for her ignoring me. I thought she was still not a friend of mine, else she would have remembered, and in that case, I needed to put in extra efforts to be her friend for life.

All the way along the rain-washed track, the sound of loose mud beneath the tires was audible. I heard a noise akin to music but kept riding. At first, I thought it must be some wood-chimes in the tires. A few seconds later, I realized that the noise was not only traveling with me, but was far too regular to be caused by the wind. I immediately applied the brakes to check the sound from the back tire. I stepped down to check, and to my surprise, I found a piece of paper tied to my seat. I pulled it and was about to throw it away, when I saw my name written on it. I let the cycle lean on me and opened the letter.

It was from Ashima:

'The way you were waiting outside the school, I was sure your index finger was a confirmation that we will be cycling together, but Mr Kartik, I am a girl who can change fate, and here I changed it again.'

Her letter brought a smile to my face. At least she noticed me waiting outside and now I had a letter from her, which I could always call my first love letter. I folded it and carefully put it in my pocket.

She reached outside her colony when I arrived cycling. Without stopping, I moved along with a beatific smile on my face. She smiled back and then softly waved her left hand, avoiding Seema or the others.

When she looked at me, it was as if every ounce of breath was taken from my lungs floating into the air like the winter fog. When she waved at me, it felt like the world had stopped, leaving just the two of us to wander the earth together. She was a story which I never wanted to end. I had heard about first love, but I realized how beautiful the feeling was only when I experienced it myself.

I reached home, put down my bag and went inside the washroom, standing in front of the mirror. I smiled looking at myself and then I brought my right hand in front. The hand which she had touched that day. I kissed my palm as if I was kissing her. I was blushing; my face turned red, as if I was standing in front of her.

I brought my face closer to the mirror and spoke softly, "Kartik, you are in love."

"Kartik, wash your hands and come for lunch." I snapped back to reality hearing my mummy shouting from outside. I didn't want to wash off her touch. Finally, I opened the door, having washed only my left hand.

I took a seat at the table. My mummy was continually speaking about some or the other thing, but I could not register anything. My ears were in a different world, hearing a different song.

I looked at my lunch, which consisted of my favourite chhole, rice, and dried chilies. Bug-eyed, I wanted to have it fast. I picked up the spoon to pour the curry over the rice, but then I stopped. I'd need to wash my right hand if I were to eat with it. Ashima's touch would also get washed off. With a pained face, I stopped and then started eating with my left hand, using a spoon.

My mummy stood to open the main door as the doorbell rang. Still sitting in my chair, I tried to see who was at the door. It was Papa; he had come early that day.

"How come you are so early today?" Mummy questioned Papa, and also started serving him the food. Papa replied from the washroom, washing his hands.

"There is work to be done at night in office at night, so I'll rest in the daytime."

Papa came near the dining table and started wiping his hands, "Kartik, how was your day in school?"

"Very nice, Papa." He took a seat next to my mother and in front of me.

"Hope your mathematics teachers are good? You need to score more in maths, else you will not be able to get maths as your subject. And you know we want the second engineer in our family after me," he smiled and so did I.

My aim in life was to become an engineer like my father, and I was already working towards my goal. "Papa, I was reading – one company Amazon.com has launched a device which contains ninety thousand books and all the newspapers in it. Can you buy that for me?"

Papa took a bite and replied, still chewing, "Aisa bhi kuch hota hai, ye kab aa gaya *and what is its name?*"

"It's known as Kindle, but I am not sure if it is available in India. But you can always ask if someone in your organization can get it from the US," I requested him, taking another spoon full of rice in my mouth. But my mother noticed me and interrupted.

"Why are you eating with your left hand? Is your right hand okay?"

With the quizzical expression on my face, I casually said, "Nothing Mummy, got hurt in school while playing."

"Oh! My god, show me what happened to you. Is this the same hand that got fractured? I told you to take care of that, but you never listen," Mummy stood up to check my hand. With an expressionless face, I was confused about what to do, when my father called my mother.

"Renuka, listen to me."

Mummy immediately turned to hear what Papa was saying. They said something to each other with their eyes, and without further checking my hand, mummy went back to her seat and started eating her food.

"Take some more rice, Kartik, you're at a growing age. You must eat more," Mummy said as she took her seat.

I never understood how they both managed to talk with their eyes. It was not the first time. I had seen Mummy conveying a message without speaking many times, and Papa correctly understanding what she wanted to say.

After finishing my lunch, I went back to my room, switched on my music system and lay down on my bed.

My room was big, with a single bed at the centre. My study table next to the bed was full of books. The front wall was covered with big and small posters of Salman, Backstreet Boys, and Shania Twain.

I lay buried in my bed, with a video game in my hands, when Papa knocked and entered. I pulled myself up as he walked in.

"What are you doing my boy?" he came next to my bed and took a seat on the chair in front of my study table.

"All well, Papa…"

He moved his eyes in all directions to take a glance of my room and then continued, "Today I came early so thought I'd sit with you and chat for a while, hope it's okay with you."

"Ya, it's perfectly fine Papa. Please tell me."

With a little smile and blush on his face, Papa continued, "Well, today when I saw you eating with the left hand, it reminded me of something funny. And as you are grown up now, I thought I could share it with you."

Now I sat up and started listening with excitement and fear while he continued.

"You know, Mummy and I had a love marriage eighteen years back."

"Yes, I know," I smiled, and he continued.

"When I touched your mom's hand for the first time in Robertson College, Jabalpur, I did not wash my hand for a week. After a week's time, your grandfather called me as my results were out, and I could not manage to score high. He asked me to present my hands in front so that he could punish me with a stick and when he saw my hand…" Papa stopped, and looked into my eyes.

"Then what happened Papa, you were hurt a lot?"

Papa placed his hand on my forehead to continue, "He dropped his stick and hugged me, saying my son's grown up today…"

Papa paused and then stood up. I thought for a while and then questioned, "Then what happened, Papa? You told him about Mummy?"

Papa turned back to me and this time took a seat on my bed, just next to me, "Your grandfather narrated how he hadn't washed his hands for a month and I kept listening."

And we both laughed out loud. He suddenly stopped and with a pause replied, "Kartik, today you are grown up, and I am proud of you. But remember one thing in life, the most precious thing in life is your partner. Tomorrow you will leave us, but your Mummy and I will be together until our last breath.

Friendship is the start, but togetherness is the end." He concluded after a minute, "Before leaving I'll only tell you, my father didn't wash his hand for months for your Dadi, and I didn't for your mother. Life takes the same circle with every generation, only the faces and environment changes."

Papa left the room, with a smile on his face. I had found a friend that day in my Papa, and I started respecting him more for that.

That year went by and I transformed from a friend to an excellent friend of Ashima's. That year passed by sharpening pencils, again and again, to take a look at her, that year passed by cycling together, that year passed by murmuring in the library, that year passed by waving when no one was watching us, that year passed by dreaming about her, that year passed by admiring her.

I opened my eyes to find Ashima standing next to me.

"Why are you sleeping like this? Come to our room," Ashima questioned rubbing her eyes.

I placed the book back to the side and went to our bedroom. To sleep next to her, holding her hands again.

5

The first three months were completed, and Ashima was now more relaxed and had adjusted to the changes in her body. I loved that time with her, planning for our baby and our future. She was feeling much better by then.

That night, I was sitting on my study table and writing something when Ashima came with a glass of water, "Hey Teddy, what are you writing?"

"Nothing."

"You are writing something. Tell me what you are up to?" she again questioned coming closer to check. I hid what I was doing with the register.

"You are hiding it from me! Please show me what you are writing." Seeing her angry frown, I decided to show her, though I had wanted it to be a surprise.

"Okay dear, I will tell you about this, but will not show you. Is that fine?"

Hearing me, she took a seat next to me on the bed carefully. I helped her place her feet up.

"I am writing letters to our baby every month of the pregnancy."

"What?"

I took a pause, turned towards her and explained, "I want my baby to know what I was feeling and what his or her mother had undergone during these nine months, so I am writing a letter every month."

"Oh my god! Teddy, you are so cute."

She gave a beatific smile and continued, "But I will read them for sure when you are not at home." She tried to be a little naughty, biting her lower lip.

"No one knows you better than me, my Angel, and this the reason I bought this today." I pulled open the drawer to show her a small sandalwood box, which had a small lock inbuilt with a little key.

With brooding eyes she said, "You can't do this Teddy, I am your love, let me read them."

"I am doing this because I love you. Some smiles are meant for a surprise and a selfie with a surprised smile is the best one." I smiled and continued, "I will be placing the letters in this box, and will hand over its key to you when you arrive with our baby. So that you can read them to him or her."

Ashima moved her head closer to me. She leaned in so that her forehead rested against mine. I closed my eyes.

"Thank you, Teddy," she said in barely more than a whisper.

"For what?" I replied in a low and husky voice.

"For being you."

Ashima gently leaned and kissed my warm lips. Love is like a baby, which takes its own time to mature into the most beautiful fruit ever. Today kissing my love seemed so simple, but it's me who knows what I have gone through to get my love in my arms.

"Oh! I am feeling too tired, Teddy," Ashima tried to turn on the bed.

"Let me help you, baby." I stood up from my chair and helped her to lie down, adjusting her pillow. I switched off the lights and took my place next to her. The table lamp with yellow light was still switched on, giving the room a soft, warm glow. I removed my spectacles and placed them back on the desk. Her pregnancy was in the thirteenth week, and by this time, her appetite and bump had started to increase rapidly. She had said goodbye to the nausea of the first trimester and felt ravenous most of the time.

I started adjusting the fringe of her hair which always attracted me to her. I began to massage her forehead softly. She closed her eyes, feeling relaxed and I continued, unblinkingly looking at my love.

I kept looking at her and started thinking about our past again.

April 2008

It was Sunday when I heard the news that our tenth CBSE board results were out. My face suddenly turned dull and tense. I started biting my nails. Wearing my bathroom slippers, I rushed to the kitchen to Mummy, shouting, "Mummy, I am going to school now, my results are out."

"*Oh! Really.* Hai Bhagwaan bache ka dhayan rakhna. *Kartik's Papa, please listen, his results are out,*" Mummy shouted to Papa, who was busy in our garden. Hearing her, Papa also rushed inside in his usual Sunday pyjamas and white vest.

"*Hey, Kartik, let me take you to school on my scooter,*" Papa immediately started washing his hands.

"*Thanks, Papa. I am waiting for you outside,*" I replied and rushed outside. Within no time my father was out with the scooter keys. My mother appeared along with him, with a bowl full of curd.

"*Have this, curd and sugar. It will bring good luck to you,*" Mummy said pouring a spoonful in my mouth. Papa started the scooter, and I hopped on. My mummy was still giving me spoonsful of curd as Papa started the scooter.

"*Mummy, let us go now. I've had enough,*" I replied taking the last spoon. Papa looked more tensed than me. His wish to see me as an engineer was quite visible in his eyes. My heartbeat was increasing with every mile that brought us closer to school.

"*You go inside and check, I'll park the scooter and come,*" Papa told me as soon as we reached. I rushed to the notice board section in my school. I crossed the corridor. Some of my batchmates were also walking rapidly with their friends and family. It was a big day for us – a day which would be declaring our future.

Soon I reached the notice board and found a bunch of students struggling to find their roll numbers. Without waiting for the crowd to clear, I pushed myself into it and started looking for my roll number, moving my finger on the glass covered noticeboard.

Everyone was shouting, hooting around me. Then I found my name and saw 97% marked against it. I turned with a smile, with a confident expression and discovered my Papa standing at some distance with a smile and tense eyes. I rushed to him and hugged him, "Papa, it's 97%."

"Great, my son, so proud of you!" Papa patted my back. I could see the happiness on his face.

"Hey Kartik, how much did you score? And namaste, uncle."

I could hear Ashima behind me. I turned and found her standing behind me, wearing a sky blue frock, her hair open, with a roll of paper in her hand. I took a step towards her, smiling, "I scored 97%. What about you?"

"Mine is 97.7%. I scored a point seven percent more than you," she replied with a glazed look.

"I was really worried till I saw my results."

"Me too. My mom wanted to come along, but I rushed off with Seema's father in her car."

As we chatted, unknowing that my father had taken a few steps back, with a smile on his face and tears of happiness in his eyes. He was always a fun father. He loved me, and for him I was a small kid, but that day he knew I was grown up. I was growing up in my life.

After waiting for a few minutes, he interrupted from behind, "Kartik, I am going home, you stay with your friends. Hope you will manage to come home by yourself?"

Hearing his voice, I turned, but before I could reply, Ashima said, "Uncle, we will come walking. I too live nearby." I could not respond to anything but just looked at her, while my father smiled and nodded before leaving.

After spending an hour in school, chatting and enjoying with friends, we both decided to walk back home. We both started walking on the quiet road of Chakrata. Tiny chunks of wood fell to the leaf litter below, the sound dissipating into the woodland around. A year back I was admiring her, days back was loving her, and that day, I was walking by her side.

"So which subject stream are you planning to opt for?" I questioned her while walking.

"I am clear about it. Arts. I am not at all interested in science or mathematics, nor do I want to be an engineer or doctor. I want to be a school teacher and a homemaker," she replied with a smile and continued, "And what about you, Kartik?"

I was sure that I was going to opt for mathematics and would be going to be an engineer, but I wanted to be with her forever. And something happened to my mind that day, and I replied, "Still thinking, not sure about it yet."

"Then you also take Arts, we will enjoy a lot. Same class, mast time pass hoga," she replied with a radiant smile on her face. I was smiling at her, but my mind was fearful. My mind was confused. At that time of my life, love was more significant for me than my career. At that time of my life, my love became bigger than the expectations of my father.

After nine years, I regretted my decision when I see my relation with my father, but I felt happy looking at Ashima beside me. I removed my hand from her forehead as she had fallen asleep. I stood to complete my third letter to my baby. I had taken the next day off from office as she had an ultrasound scheduled. The nine months of pregnancy were bringing back the past nine years spent with her, and I was loving those nostalgic moments.

6

We entered the ultrasound room in Apollo Hospital in Noida. It was a small room, with a single bed and an ultrasound machine. With dim lights and monitors, it seemed as if we were going to see our baby live.

The doctor asked Ashima to lie on the bed. I could feel her fear and excitement simultaneously.

"You may leave your husband's hand, Ashima, nothing to worry about the ultrasound," the doctor told Ashima, pulling her top, exposing her stomach which was slightly enlarged by then. I took a step back at a position to keep an eye on the monitor as well as on Ashima.

The doctor poured some serum on her stomach and asked the nurse to switch off the lights. The doctor then picked up a transducer probe and started moving it on her stomach. Ashima was smiling as it was cold and ticklish. Soon we could see the black and white image on the monitor. I was stressing my eyes to get the precise image of our baby, but I could only make out a hazy picture.

"Look at this point; this is your baby. Yes, this white moving spot," the doctor confirmed, placing her finger on the screen.

"Oh! So sweet, my baby," Ashima replied with a beatific smile on her face. I took a step towards her to hold her hand again. It was the most breathtaking event of my life. I could feel the presence of our love; I could feel the baby's presence around us. Ashima was pressing my wrist with every movement of the baby on the screen.

"So, what you both are expecting, a girl or a boy?" the doctor asked with a smile, continuing marking some lines on the screen.

"It must be a girl, beautiful like Ashima," I replied.

Ashima immediately interrupted, "No, it must be handsome like my Teddy, my boy."

The doctor smiled and continued making some notes, "Let's see who will win."

The doctor then shifted her probe to the lower part of the stomach. She was trying to find something; I am not sure what, but suddenly her smile converted to a tense face. She was marking some spots and measurements on the screen. My eyes were on her and the display, whereas Ashima was still smiling looking at the baby.

"Is everything fine, doctor?" I asked

The doctor asked the nurse to clean Ashima's stomach and shifted her chair toward the desk, searching some intercom number on the paper placed.

"You may take Ashima to Dr Sangeeta; I will be informing her on the phone."

"Is everything fine, ma'am?" I again questioned.

"Nothing to worry." This time she smiled and replied. I then helped Ashima to step down from the bed, and we started moving downstairs to meet Dr Sangeeta holding hands.

"He is so cute, my Chhota Teddy," Ashima said with a curious smile on her face.

"No, she is so cute, meri Chhoti Ashima," I retorted. She then pinched me on my shoulder to win the argument. But then she stopped, closed her eyes and presented her two fingers in front of me.

"Oh! Not again Ashima," I replied showing an irritated face.

"Pick one fast or say, it's Chhota Teddy."

"Never, let me pick one," I replied and picked her middle finger this time.

"Yes! Yes! Yes! It's Chhota Teddy. I was always sure," she replied with excitement. I continued walking, giving her a glazed look. She followed me smiling as we reached outside Dr Sangeeta's cabin. I knocked on the door and opened it slightly.

"Ya, please come in, Kartik," Dr Sangeeta responded from inside, sitting on her chair. I kept holding the door and allowed Ashima to enter first. We took our seat and handed over the file to her.

"Okay, so I just got a call from the doctor who did your ultrasound."

I looked a little tensed after reading her face.

"Is everything fine, doctor?" I questioned, interrupting her.

"Nothing to worry as of now. But yes, time to take precautions." She slightly leaned back on her chair to speak to us and continued.

"Ultrasound suspects a disorder of the placenta," she replied and before I could ask more she took her pen and paper to explain, "Placenta is the organ which is attached to the womb and provides nourishment for the growing baby. Your placenta is near or lying across the cervix, i.e., the neck of the womb, and it can block the baby's way out."

"Is it serious, what should we do now?" I immediately questioned, holding Ashima's hand. Ashima lost her smile hearing this.

"Nothing to worry. If the placenta is low in the womb, there is a higher chance of bleeding during pregnancy and to avoid that, Ashima must remain in complete bed rest now," she confirmed.

"Bed rest means, I can't even go to the kitchen or washroom?" Ashima interrupted.

"Not exactly like that. But yes, try to rest more. Avoid working in the kitchen or cleaning the house or long drives. It would be better if you call someone to help – your mother or Kartik's mother. Someone needs to be with you. I know Kartik can't be with you all the time."

"Sure, ma'am. We will make some arrangement," I confirmed. The doctor wrote down some medicines, and then we stood up to go home.

I was more cautious about Ashima, so I asked her to walk slowly. And I also drove the car at the speed of not more than twenty kmph.

"With this speed, we will reach home tomorrow, Kartik."

"Be quiet Ashima, you need to be cautious, and we have to plan things now. Till now, we have not informed any of our parents that you are pregnant. The first thing we need to do is inform them and then ask your mom to come and stay with us," I replied, still driving slowly on the empty road of Noida.

"My mom can't come, you know; she is busy handling Sheenu, while Bhabhi goes to office," Ashima said.

Ashima's mother needed to take care of Sheenu, her elder brother Rohit's son, while Rohit and his wife Priya went to work.

"We need to call your mom, Kartik."

"But you know, she will not come without Papa from Dehradun. And you also know he doesn't like you, nor would he like to stay with me," I replied with a grave look.

"I know he doesn't like me, but he will be happy hearing that he is going to be a grandfather. I am sure everything will be fine," Ashima assured me.

"How can you be so understanding, when I am so tensed?" I showed my concern.

"They are our parents, Kartik, and I will be happy with them. And who knows, because of our baby, the misunderstanding may be forgotten."

Ashima knew how to get me to agree to everything, and she was an expert at that. My father, who was once my role model and best friend, was left far behind in the relationship as I grew up from a boy to a man. My relation with my father started going downhill after my tenth class result. A space had grown between us, which I could never bridge.

I still remember the day when I was leaving for school after my tenth class results to opt for subjects. And I was excited as I was sure I was going to take maths for my engineering.

"You will be getting the subject for your choice easily, my boy. Tonight we will have a grand party for your first stepping stone to becoming an engineer."

Papa patted my back while I was sitting on the sofa tying my shoelaces.

"I will make chicken kababs tonight, your papa's favourite," Mummy replied sitting in front of me.

"Why Papa's? You must cook my favourite as I studied harder," I replied standing adjusting my jeans.

"Okay beta, will make your favorite egg curry as well. Happy now?" Mummy replied smiling.

I picked up my documents and said goodbye.

"Enjoy your day beta, we will be waiting for the party tonight," Papa waved from behind as I cycled out of the gate. I waved back with a big smile on my face. Soon, I reached school and found a line of students outside the principal's room, opting for our subjects. I stood behind Raghav who was last in the queue.

"Hey, Raghav, which subject you are planning to take?"

"I am taking commerce, and you?" he replied and questioned back.

"Science with maths," I replied.

"You always wanted maths; you told me before as well."

"Ya, maths is something I love, and I want to go for engineering in the future," I was replying to Raghav when I saw Ashima, coming out of the principal's cabin with a big broad smile on her face. She was dressed in a yellow and orange salwar suit, with an orange scarf. She looked beautiful and different that day. She was wearing silver earrings, had her hair open, with light pink lipstick on her soft pink lips. I knew I loved her, but when I saw her that day, I felt as if space and time became the finest imaginable, as if time collapsed into one speck and exploded at the speed of light. It felt like she was my universe. My mind started thinking; I could run forever, search forever, but in the end, every path would lead back to her heart and soul because she was the one whom I loved, she was the one I'd die for.

"Hey, Ashima, which subjects?" I shouted at her, still in the queue.

She turned to me and came running. "Arts, I told you before."

I congratulated her, and before I could speak further, she excused herself as she wanted to talk to some of our batchmates who would be joining her in the same class. For a moment I felt alone, and began to wonder, what if I were to lose her forever.

As soon as we met, I knew she was the one. The one I would spend my days thinking of and the one I would spend my nights dreaming about. The one who would hold me when I would cry and the one who would laugh with me. The one who I would share my life with and the one I would love forever in my life. But at that moment of my life, I felt I was going to lose her forever. I was afraid that she'd find someone better than me in a new class, or amongst new batchmates, or maybe during her further studies.

Soon, we would be sitting in different classes, soon she would go to a different college for further studies, and I would go for mine. Soon distance would separate us, soon communication would be less frequent. Soon I would not find her near me, soon I would not see her everyday. Would I be able to win her heart?

I got confused with so many thoughts in my head. On the one hand, there was Ashima, my love. On the other was Papa, my role model. I was not bothered about my career then, but worried about how to make my father understand. I was worried about not letting her go. I was concerned about losing her forever.

And then I took a decision, which changed one relation forever. I opted for Arts.

I knew my father was angry with me, but I was not sure he would continue to be so for seven years. Now, after nine years, I never regretted taking Arts. After being in the marketing industry, I knew I was always meant for this. I enjoyed my job. Maybe my love for engineering was the love of my father which had overshadowed my own interests.

7

It was nine in the night, and after dinner, we sat in the balcony. The weather was perfect that night, with a soft breeze blowing. Although summers where about to start, the breeze was cool, due to unexpected showers in Delhi.

Ashima picked up her mobile and dialled a number.

"Whom you are calling?" I asked making myself comfortable on the wooden chair.

"Calling your mom, Teddy. Let us inform her and ask her to come," she replied.

"Are you sure, Ashima? You know the problem with Papa."

She disconnected the phone and replied, "I know he is angry with you because you married me, but if this is the only reason, let me handle it."

"It's not only because of you; I know you can handle him. It's me who feels guilty for not meeting his expectations," I replied.

Hearing me, Ashima leaned toward me and questioned with a soft voice, "Are you guilty for marrying me?"

"How can you even think that way?" I questioned her back and kissed on her forehead. "It's more than just marriage for me, Angel." I took a pause and continued, "I don't know what happened and why it happened, maybe it was my fault or it was Papa's fault, but the distance that was created between us, kept on growing."

"And the reason is me, na?" Ashima replied with a dull face.

"Never. I always told you, it's not you," I again confirmed before continuing.

"Do you remember the day, Ashima, when we took our subjects in school?" I started telling Ashima, while she listened brooding.

"That day, I came to know that you were planning to go get ice cream with Seema and a few other classmates. You invited me as well. Do you remember that?"

"Hun! I remember, and we went nearest ice cream parlor where we all had fun till seven in the evening," Ashima confirmed.

"Yes, the same day. When I returned home at around eight and pressed the doorbell, I was tense and downcast. My face had turned red in fear. I wanted to run away as I had done the unexpected for not only Papa, but for myself as well.

"I pressed the doorbell again, and after a few minutes, Mummy opened the door, and without listening to me, she slapped me hard. I shouted, 'Sorry Mummy, sorry I took Arts because I want to do something different. Sorry Mummy, please forgive me.'

"Tears rolled down my eyes and my face turned red. I tried to safeguard my face hiding behind both my hands, while Mummy slapped me again.

"Mummy kept hitting me on my back and cheeks and told me that Papa was very tensed as I hadn't returned from school in the afternoon. He went to look for me on his scooter. He tried to look at me at many places. His blood pressure increased, and he fell off his scooter and broke his elbow.

"Hearing her, I rushed inside to my Papa's bedroom and found him standing at the door with his right hand plastered. With tears in my eyes, I asked him how he was? How was he feeling then? But he kept standing in front of me with no expressions and no words. His red eyes answered that he knew that I had taken Arts and his dream to see me as an engineer had been shattered.

"Since then, I tried on many occasions to gel back with him, but he never spoke a single word to me. Later, he found out my reason for shattering his dream, and so he hates you too."

I stood up from my chair and walked to the corner of the balcony and continued, "You know, Ashima, some relations are like mobiles, which are out of network when you need them the most."

Hearing me, Ashima interrupted, "Teddy, when the network creates a problem, we change the network, not our mobile." She then paused to explain, "To mend your relation with Papa, we need to change the situation, and not hide from them. Our baby will bring this change in him. Allow me to call them?"

I then turned to look at her with a grave look, and she dialled my mummy's number.

"Turn on the speaker phone," I told her.

"Hello," Mummy replied after a few rings. Her voice sounded old and frail.

"Hello, Mummyji, it's me Ashima."

"Oh! Ashima beta, how you are you and how is Kartik?"

"We both are fine Mummyji, and how are you both? You sound dull?" Ashima replied

"We are fine betaji. Just have a little cough and cold."

Ashima took a pause and then continued, "We have news for you."

"What happened, is everything fine?"

"Yes, everything fine. Actually, you are soon going to become a grandmother," Ashima answered slowly.

"What? Wow! I am so thankful to the Almighty. So, I will be getting a Chhota Kartik now." Mummy, replied with pleasure and shouted to Papa, saying, "*Sunte ho*, Ashima is pregnant."

"May god listen to you," Ashima added and continued with a pause, "Mummyji, there is but a small problem."

"What happened? Tell me," Mummy questioned.

Ashima informed Mummy about the complication she was facing and asked her if she could come to Noida and stay with us. Mummy took a pause and replied, "Nothing to worry, betaji, these are minor problems during pregnancy."

Mummy continued after some thought, "Let me discuss this with your Papa and will let you know our plans."

"Sure Mummy," Ashima replied

"And where is my Kartik, let me congratulate him," Mummy asked. But I was feeling shy to talk to her at that moment, and I gestured to Ashima that I didn't want to.

"He is still on his way home Mummy, got late today," Ashima handled my request correctly.

As she disconnected the call, I hugged her and kept hugging her for some time.

"Missing Papa?" Ashima questioned, massaging me softly on my back.

"I miss him a lot, Ashima. He was my role model; he was my best friend. I miss my childhood days with him; I miss those moments when we used to laugh as a family. I miss those hugs from him," I replied getting emotional.

"I can understand Teddy, but do not worry, everything will be fine one day."

Being an only child, my father had always been my best friend. He never scolded me and tried to understand me as much as possible. He was my biggest supporter ever, and I missed him for that.

I don't know how and when our relation reached such a point, but I felt it was me who was responsible for it, but the fact was I could choose any worse thing for me, for my love, my Ashima.

Next day, we tried to arrange a full-time maid at home, who could help Ashima in my absence, while we kept waiting for a call back from Mummy.

Few days passed before we had a call on Sunday morning. I was on my study table writing the fourth letter to my baby when the doorbell rang. Ashima was on the bed reading a book. I asked her to relax and went to the door. To my surprise, Mummy and Papa were standing in front of me. I was shocked, but recovered quickly. I smiled and touched their feet. Mummy hugged me and kissed me, while Papa went inside without saying a word to me.

I picked up the suitcase and welcomed Mummy. "By which train did you come, Mummy? You should have informed me."

"We came by car, Kartik. Your Papa drove," Mummy replied and then questioned, "Where is Ashima?"

"Oh! Really?" I replied and continued. "She is resting inside, Mummy; please come in."

Mummy followed me to the bedroom, and as she entered, Ashima tried to get up from the bed to touch her feet. Mummy stopped her and said, "You are exempted from this, beta, no need to touch my feet."

Ashima laughed and hugged Mummy. Ashima and Mummy then went out to the living room where Papa was seated. She was about to touch his feet when he stopped her saying, "Let it be, it's perfectly okay."

"How was your journey, Papa?" Ashima questioned and took a seat.

"It was okay," Papa replied.

I could see how curt Papa was to Ashima, but she kept smiling and conversing with him. I didn't know how to make Papa normal and make him forgive me.

"Let me make tea for everyone," I stood and moved to the kitchen.

"You wait, let me make it," Mummy asked me to stop, but I stopped her and went to serve them. I also wanted to avoid Papa, whose eyes were making me drown in guilt.

I stayed in the kitchen, struggling with my inner feelings, until Ashima walked inside.

"Hey, why have you come here? Go and rest," I said.

Ashima walked inside and stood in front of me, taking the support of the kitchen platform. She looked relaxed and was smiling.

"What? What happened? Why are you smiling?" I questioned.

She placed her both arms around my neck and then gave me a naughty smile, "You are hiding from Papa, na?"

I tried to avoid her question, but she waited for my answer, "Yes. I don't know how to make things cordial with Papa."

Something was cooking in Ashima's mind, and it was quite visible to me looking at her face. So I questioned her, "What? Again, you are looking at me differently."

Whenever she looked at me smiling with sly eyes, I knew something was going on in her mind.

"Do you remember Teddy, how you convinced me about your love?" Ashima questioned

"Of course baby."

"Was I not a stranger to you?"

"I knew you; we were in the same class," I replied instantly.

"But I was not someone whom you knew since many years?"

I nodded to show my agreement.

"Your father is known to you since you were born. He was your best friend back in time. When you can convince me, whom you hardly met, why can't you get your Papa to see eye to eye, the person who loves you so much," she explained, stressing my strengths.

I felt she was right and her words were my strength. She always knew how to boost my inner power.

I took the tea on a tray and Ashima helped me with some snacks to serve. We returned to my parents. I took a seat pulling out the dining table chair, while Ashima sat next to Mummy, and started the conversation. Papa was silent and was sipping tea in between. Neither did he look at me, nor did I try to start a conversation with him.

But my mind was working on how to break the ice. By the time we completed our tea, the maid arrived. Ashima gave her instructions about the dinner, while Mummy and Papa went to their room to freshen up.

"Angel, I am going down to the park for sometime, you want me to bring something?" I questioned Ashima as I wanted to run away from facing Papa for sometime and be by myself.

Ashima looked at me with a sarcastic smile. She replied, "Okay, bring some apples. Papa loves eating apples every morning."

"Sure," I smiled and went downstairs.

She understood me better than anyone else did. I was sure after a few years we both would also start interacting with our eyes as my parents did.

I bought some apples and went to the park. I sat down on a bench and pondered about what Ashima had explained to me. She was correct. I started thinking about the day when I had proposed to her and began to hatch my plan to make my father reconcile with me.

I remember it was a most terrible task for me to propose to Ashima, although I was her best friend after we completed our school and joined Birla Institute of Management in Greater Noida.

Ashima's parents shifted to Greater Noida, whereas I stayed in the hostel. But she being a local was a big help to me. Every weekend I'd have lunch at her home. As for her parents, I was already a family member.

I was always worried, wondering if her parents might start thinking of me as her brother and this tension was urging me to propose to her fast. On the other hand, my fear of losing her forever because of the proposal was choking me. I was in deep trouble and could not understand what to do.

One evening, I was going back from the hostel mess when I saw a girl standing next to her scooty reading a greeting card. I kept looking at her and then a plan hatched in my mind. I immediately ran to my room..

I pulled out a card sheet, folded it like a greeting card and wrote a beautiful line on it with sketch pens: "I feel my heart stops beating when you are not near, and it beats very fast when you are around. Is it love or just a blood pressure problem?"

I was ready with the card, but somewhere in my heart, I was worried. My thoughts with questions and answers were all jumbled in my mind. I could hardly blink my eyes shut that night.

The next day, I tied the card to the handle of her scooty, when she was attending a class. Most of the time I was praying, wiping my sweat and drinking water in tension, hiding at a distance. My heart was beating fast as I saw her. She was wearing a blue suit that day, holding her bag. I had not written my name, but was still worried about rejection.

She placed her bag on her scooty and saw the card. She looked at it and read it with a dreamy look. She folded the card back, placed it in the bag, and left. I remained standing in surprise as I was expecting something different. I was confused at her lack of reaction and could not understand what my move should be. What if she took it as a letter from someone else? And then after a few minutes, my mobile rang. It was Ashima. My heart stopped and everything went still for me. My eyes could see only her name flashing on the screen. Should I pick her call or not? It seemed like Judgment day for me.

"Hey Ashima, hello," I said, trying to be normal.

"Where are you? Come urgently to the auditorium."

She disconnected the call after just one line. The auditorium was on the other side of the campus, and I walked to the place, full of confusion and fear. I could see her scooty outside.

It was evening time, and the auditorium was almost empty. I could hear the sound of my tapping shoes while I kept looking for her. I dialled her number and found her mobile ringing on the first floor. As I reached upstairs, I saw her standing at the center of the hall, facing another side.

"Hey Ashima, you called me. What are you doing here?" It was tough for me to behave normal, but I tried my best.

She turned to question with a grave look, "Since how many years have you known me, Kartik?"

I looked afraid, and replied in fear, "Four years." Listening to my answer, she moved closer to me and presented her two fingers.

"Pick one."

I kept looking into her eyes, and without looking at her fingers, I picked one. She smiled and hugged me, which was unexpected. Coming closer to my ears, she spoke softly, "I know your handwriting, Teddy, since our school days, and both fingers say you love me as much as I do."

It was the perfect gift for me, as I tightened my arms to hug her. That evening was the most memorable for me. For that day, for those words, I'd give everything of my life.

She stepped back again, and I stared deep into her eyes. Gaining all strength in my heart, I cupped her cheek that was slowly turning red. I smiled at her before slowly leaning forward. My other hand was shaking slightly, while my mind was saying the same sentence over and over, "I love you, I love you." But with the sound of my heart beating so loudly, I couldn't concentrate. I felt like it was going to explode.

Finally, my lips touched her. Sparks flew in every direction, and the world slowly disappeared around us. It was a short yet warm kiss. I honestly never knew a kiss so innocent could make me feel out of the universe and could realize the purpose of my life.

That day our friendship got over, and our love story began. I started being her companion because we loved each others' company. I started looking at her closely because I could not find anyone more beautiful than her. I started loving her more, as I knew no one could love me more than her.

Confessing that we loved each other was fascinating, and the kiss was a blunder for us, as we still remembered each other as school-going friends. But the chemical changes in our body would not let us be children anymore, and kissing became our energy tonic.

The greeting card had helped me to propose to my love, and I started making a plan to bring back Papa with the same idea. I was thankful to my Angel for showing me the path.

8

I planned to start communication with Papa the same way, but this time, Ashima was on my side. We tried to observe Papa's daily routine at our place. Every morning, he went to the central park for a walk, followed by yoga with Mummy, sitting on the same bench every day. I monitored him for the next few days from a distance.

Ashima suggested I make a card myself as it would connect to him better than a bought one.

That night, I made a beautiful card with smileys inside a palm and wrote these lines: "Walked holding your hand, and you were the reason for the smile on my face."

Ashima suggested I place that card on the same bench in the park where he did his yoga. Everything went according to plan. I went to the central park just before Papa was about to leave, early in the morning. I tied that card to the seat. I walked behind the small Mother Dairy shop to keep an eye on him. I saw him completing his walk, so I dialled Ashima's number, "Angel, Papa is on his way to the bench where I've tied the card."

"Great! Keep me updated. Did he find the card?" she questioned. "Reply Teddy. Did he check?"

"Wait Angel, he has not noticed it yet," I replied.

"Papa has sat down and has closed his eyes," I informed Ashima.

"What? Is he sleeping in the park?"

"No, foolish girl. He is doing some yoga asana," I replied

"You called me foolish? You are foolish. I am putting the phone back, do it yourself!" Ashima replied in anger.

"Hey Angel, sorry dear. How can you be foolish?"

"First give me a kiss, then only I will talk to you," she replied naughtily.

"What! I am too tensed right now, and you want a kiss?"

'Yes, kiss me now," she insisted. Hearing her, I kissed my phone.

"Now it's better, and please relax," she replied with a laugh.

"Ashima, he just picked up the card. Papa is reading it," I replied excitedly.

"Now what? Tell me his reaction," Ashima questioned. "Tell me, Teddy?"

"I don't know. He read it and threw it away," I replied, disappointed

"Hey, cheer up! You are not going to succeed in the first attempt. You need to keep trying."

I thought for a while. "I think, you are correct, but it will be more awkward for me to face him now."

"Hey! C'mon, he is your father. Just a little angry and nothing else. By the way, you have not mentioned your name on the card," Ashima tried to calm me.

"Ya, that's true. I think he might finally realize it's me when he receives one every day," I replied.

"Yes, and when he realizes how much you love him, he will hug you, my Teddy." Ashima boosted my confidence.

Convincing Papa was not an easy task. He was not only angry because I took Arts, but somehow felt that Ashima had taken me away from him. I was everything for him, and he had devoted his entire life for me. And when I chased Ashima, he thought I was forgetting my career. He could never differentiate my relationship with Ashima and himself. That was the reason he hated Ashima as well. For him, Ashima took me away from him and my career. Although I was working in the Global Marketing company and earning well, he always felt, I would have done better being an engineer. Some relationships must be left in turmoil, as unwrapping them brings more confusion.

But Ashima had decided that she would make our family complete by bringing a smile to the faces of my Papa and me, together. That night she helped me make another greeting card with the message, 'For me, the name of the father was another name of love'.

That night we enjoyed painting the card together. Ashima painted my nails with fabric colours, and I painted her belly making a smiley. What a fun night that was! Our baby would be laughing at his crazy parents.

The next morning, I placed the card on the same bench and hid at my usual spot. I was expecting a definite reply from him, but that day, he did not even look at it, forget reading its contents before throwing it away. That certainly was no progress.

'I may be a prince, but my Dad will always be a king.'

'Those who love don't go away, but forgive our mistakes, smile and walk again.'

So this went on with the same reaction from Papa. I thought of asking Mummy, but Ashima said I must get Papa back on my own. Mummy would have already tried in these many years. I was losing my patience and my fight to get him back. I could feel the uneasiness Ashima was in, but still, to make me happy, she was there, sitting beside me every night.

And that night, I was making another card for him. I had already lost my interest and hope after trying for the last twelve days. Ashima was sitting next to me on the bed, while I was making a card sitting on my desk.

"Why don't you sleep, Angel?"

"You know na Teddy, I can't sleep without hugging you tightly," she replied making an innocent face.

"You can't hug me right now. Your stomach has grown, and our baby is in between," I said with a soft smile, continuing making my card.

"Ouch!"

"What happened? Are you okay?" I stood up anxiously.

Ashima was smiling while her eyes showed she was feeling something different. She took hold of my hand, saying in excitement, "Come… come… give me your hand."

And the way she was pressing my hand, I was sure she felt something. To confirm, I questioned her again, "Tell me Ashima, what happened?"

"He kicked, Teddy, he kicked!" she replied excitedly. Her eyes turned big with excitement. I broke into a big smile, as she took my hand and placed it on her enlarged stomach.

"Place your hand softly to the right side. He kicked here." I moved my hand softly trying to feel the kick.

"Did you feel something?" Ashima questioned softly.

"Why are you speaking so softly?" I too asked her whispering.

"He might get scared hearing our voices and won't kick," she replied again in a whisper.

"Are you mad, Ashima? My baby cannot be afraid of anyone," I confirmed in a loud voice now, and before I could continue or Ashima could reply, he kicked again with full force.

"Yes! Yes! He kicked, Angel. I could feel the baby, he kicked!"

"Teddy, hope you can feel what I am feeling now. It's just such an amazing feeling to be a mother."

"I know Angel, and I can't wait to be a father."

We both were lost in the new feeling – laughing, smiling and touching the belly to get a feel for our baby.

That whole night, he kicked, and we both continued feeling his presence among us. That night, we could feel the beginning of a new life.

That night, I wrote these lines in the letter, "I felt you for the first time from inside the womb, and since then, I've wanted to hold your hands; since then, I've wanted to hug you; since then, I love you more."

I was excited about that morning because Ashima said that that day was going to be different. She believed Papa would surely give a response. I hoped her belief would turn out to be true, but life is not as simple as we always think.

That day, I placed the card on the bench as I had been doing, and waited for his response. That day was cloudy, with a soft wind blowing and a few drops of rains. I kept hiding behind to check his reaction. As a son, I was waiting to see a smile on his face, so that I could run and hug him to say sorry.

Soon, Papa reached the same bench along with Mummy. My heartbeat was rising as if my exam results were going to be declared. He then picked up the card, looked at it, moving it to some distance from his face as if he was trying to read it. He then placed it on the bench and sat on it to complete his yoga, as the bench was wet. That day, I thought I had lost him forever. A warm teardrop rolled down my eye. I decided I'd not be making any more cards and threw the sketch pen which I was holding in my hand to walk towards Papa, crossing the iron railing. I wanted to let my heart out that day. I wanted Papa to talk about his feelings. I wanted him to know how much I missed him. I wanted to talk to him about Ashima; I wanted to bring him back. I crossed the tall palm trees and was about to reach him when the rain started pouring down. Papa and Mummy stood up from the bench and opened the umbrella and made their way towards the gate. A cold drop of rain woke me up and stopped my feet. I kept standing there, without blinking and saw the greeting card getting wet. With every drop of water, its colours were fading away, just as our relationship was. I could feel the hot and cold water on my cheeks, and then I realized I was crying.

I had everything in my life, but still felt incomplete without his blessings and his presence. I remained standing watching my writing on the card getting washed off. My belief was turning to reality, that he no longer loved me. I too was soon going to be a father and was confused about how a father could ignore his son to such an extent. That day I realized my unconditional love for him was only one-sided; he had already stopped loving me long back. I took a seat on the same bench in the rain. I picked up the wet greeting card, which already had been washed away, as had my dream to hug my father. I remained seated and decided not to show any reaction to Ashima, considering her health. I was done trying.

After an hour, I moved back home, thanks to the rain which helped me to hide my tears.

"Teddy, any good news?" Ashima asked me softly as I entered.

"No success yet, Angel." I acted normal.

She patted me softly, with a smile and replied, "Some journeys in life look like failures without knowing you are going to achieve bigger success just after one more step."

I gave a fake smile, while she continued, "You're drenched. Go and change, fast."

I nodded. Ashima followed me, and while I was changing my clothes, she continued, "I am inviting my parents tonight for dinner. You, come early from office."

"I don't think that's a good idea. Papa is here, and he will say something to your family, and then you will get tense," I replied.

"Teddy, I understand, but my Dad is insisting on meeting your parents."

After changing, I moved to her and replied with a brooding expression, "Then promise me something."

Ashima placed her hand on my right shoulder to relax her head on my left shoulder, "And promise you what, dear?"

"Whatever happens, you will not take any tension, promise me."

Ashima thought for a second and then turned my face towards her and let her lips grab mine. She didn't allow me to speak further, but made her soft, glossy lips flow seamlessly to mine. Her right hand was playing with the hair on the back of my head, and my hands were caressing her softly on her back. I then pulled her saying, "Leave me, Ashima, and stop exciting me."

She laughed loud with a naughty face, "If you find me taking tension, do what I did now and we will get lost in ourselves, forgetting the world around us."

I smiled at her idea and her knack to explain everything with a smile on her face. During the last nine years, I had never seen her worried for too long. She was a girl who found out a solution to bring her smile back, or I must say, she was a girl who couldn't live without a smile on her face.

Later, I got ready for office and left. I wondered at Papa who was not showing any change in his behaviour, even when he knew I was making greeting cards for him since the past two weeks.

The whole day, I kept thinking about Papa and the happy days spent with him. But the more I was thinking, the tenser I was getting.

That day, I returned early from office. Ashima, as usual, was resting in our room. Mummy was helping the maid in the kitchen and Papa was in his room, watching television, I suppose.

I placed the laptop on my desk, and Mummy came with a glass of water. "Thanks, Mummy."

"She is not feeling well today. I have asked her to sleep for sometime," Mummy told me.

"Why? What happened to her?"

"Not feeling comfortable, uneasiness. It happens. I've asked her to rest so that she can enjoy the dinner."

"Thanks, Mummy," I replied opening my wristwatch. Mummy went back into the kitchen.

I took a shower,and when I returned, Ashima had woken up, but was still resting in bed, looking at me. "Hey Angel, you woke up?"

She kept smiling, without replying to anything.

I removed the towel and started wearing a T-shirt and shorts, when she replied, "You were looking so cute, Teddy, and that kiss, I could never forget in my life."

I turned back to listen to her in curiosity and asked, "When, Angel?"

"You remember, we went for a picnic to Sahastra Dhara in Dehradun? That mesmerizing waterfall?"

"Oh! During our college vacations? Yes, I remember," I replied burying myself next to her, facing her.

"You were looking damn cute that day. Something happened to me seeing you open your shirt and swim topless in the water," Ashima replied.

"Did you imagine me like Mandaakini or what?"

Ashima laughed and continued, "Actually, I intentionally came into the changing room that day, knowing that you were there."

Bug-eye, I replied, "Oh shit! And you are telling me now. If you would have told me clearly, I was carrying a condom as well that day." I tried to be funny, and she punched me for that.

That was the second time we had kissed.

After I proposed to her in college, we came to Dehradun for a weekend. I planned to visit my parents while Ashima stayed with Seema. We planned to visit Sahastra Dhara, a waterfall near Rishikesh. After having fun for a few hours in the water, I decided to change and went to the changing room. It was just a small hut made up of bamboo and grass. I took my towel, and wearing only shorts, went inside. I was about to take off the shorts when Angel entered. She looked shy. So was I, but she didn't go out. She came inside and locked the door, without uttering a word. When you love someone, shyness vanishes, and I realized that for the first time. The next thing I remembered, she had slammed her lips on mine and nearly knocked all the wind from my lungs. I hardly had a moment to react before she pressed her tongue to the seam of my lips and, at my grant of access, delved inside my mouth. It was a very sloppy kiss, and the strong taste of Maggi got exchanged in the intermingling of our blowing breaths. Her arm reached up and tangled around my thick, muscular neck. In an instant, she had pulled away and arched up into my broad chest, moaning at the contact of my body heat against her own. I plunged back into her lips and when the knowledge that there were others outside moved us apart, I kept looking at her. She leaned on the bamboo wall with eyes downcast, in shyness.

I was completely unprepared. You would think after all those years I'd spent with Ashima – watching her talk, laugh and frown – I would know all there was to know about her lips. But I hadn't imagined how warm they would feel pressed against my own.

We both started our journey as friends in school. We had started off as teenagers. Being together in life was a fantastic feeling for both of us. For me, my life was just for her, and I never wanted anything else except a smile on her face.

We live once, and in one life, we breathe a million times. I wanted her to smile more than our breaths. For me, her smiles were more precious than any gem on this earth, and I would do anything for that.

"You miss our days before marriage, Teddy?" Ashima questioned while we lay side by side on our bed.

"No, because you are with me, and every new day is becoming memorable walking along with you," I replied slowly.

"Teddy, will you always love me as you do now?"

"I have loved you for half of my life, which I have lived, and there could be no reason which could stop me from loving you forever and ever," I replied, kissing her hand softly.

It was seven in the evening when the doorbell rang. We could hear from our room that it was Ashima's parents. I could hear Mummy open the door and talking to them. I stood up and so did Ashima. I helped her walk out of the room.

I touched the feet of Ashima's parents and requested them to be comfortable. Mummy informed that Papa was in the washroom and would be joining them soon. Sheenu started running from one corner to another of our house. It was going to be a good get together with Ashima's parents, brother, bhabhi and my parents here. Papa joined us after sometime. He greeted her parents and took his seat on the sofa next to her father. A conversation with my father was always a tough job for Ashima's parents.

"So, hope you are comfortable in Noida?" Ashima's papa questioned, although I could feel his hesitation in speaking to Papa.

"It's so strange when someone asks if you are feeling comfortable in your own home," Papa replied sarcastically.

"No, no I didn't mean that. I asked due to the change in the city."

"It's okay," Papa replied without any expression on his face.

Almost after thirty minutes of unfriendly conversations, Bhabi came to the rescue.

"Dinner is ready at the dining table, please join us." I stood and asked everyone to come. Papa took the center seat, followed by Ashima's father and then me. There were all vegetarian dishes as Ashima's parents were vegetarian. As everyone took their positions, Ashima and Bhabhi started to serve.

"The food is delicious. The paneer is very tasty," Ashima's mother complimented.

"Thank you; Ashima guided our maid," Mummy replied.

Papa kept thinking, and then interrupted, "A family dinner without non-vegetrian food is so dull."

"We don't eat non-vegetarian food, Bhaisahab, but it does not mean we don't enjoy ourselves," Ashima's mom replied with a smile.

But Papa took it sarcastically and replied, "My son has changed, else he would have converted Ashima to a non-vegetarian."

"It's her own choice, and I respect her for that," I tried to reply, softly taking a bite.

"Yes, I know, it's only your parents who you do not respect. *In logon ka respect to keroge hi tum,*" Papa gave a sarcastic look and replied. I looked at Ashima; she was asking me to stop responding. I too didn't want to create a scene in front of the guests, but Papa was not going to end. For him, it was an opportunity to let his heart out and make Ashima's family know that his relationship with his son had been affected because of their daughter.

"Aap ko kya fark padta hai, beta to humne khoya hai." He paused and then continued, *"Aap ki beti ke liye to badhiya ladka mila, iklauta, jisko apne maa-baap ki bhi kader nahi."*

His comment shook me from inside. How could he say that! He had almost made them seem responsible for our sour relationship. I was already burning from inside and hearing him, I could not resist myself from replying.

I left the bite I was about to take and replied, "What do you want to say? Ashima proposed to me? She intentionally married me because I am the only son of yours? You are wrong, Papa."

"You cannot talk to me like this. Don't think you can insult me just because I am at your place," Papa replied in anger.

Mummy stood from her place to intervene and requested Papa to calm down.

"Leave him, Mummy. He is not a kid who does not understand the difference between right and wrong," I shot back.

Ashima's brother tried to stop me by placing his hand on my shoulder and requested me to relax. I looked at Ashima's face, she looked tensed and was asking me to stop replying.

"Teddy, please sit and eat your food."

"Acha khasa Kartik *naam rakha tha.* She has made my son a Teddy bear," Papa threw another sarcastic comment.

I gave an annoying look, "What are you saying Papa? She calls me Teddy lovingly."

"What love? This love has spoiled your life. If you had been an engineer, you would be earning more and would be having some engineer wife."

His every word was making me angrier and provoking me to reply, "My life is not spoiled. I am happy in my life. Your aspirations to make me an engineer are not letting you be happy."

By then, Mummy had started crying. Ashima's mom stood from her seat and tried to console her. Ashima also rose from her chair and came to me and began requesting me to stop. I pushed her hand and moved closer to Papa, who by then was walking towards the drawing room.

"You have never understood me, and I realized in the morning, you will never do. Because you are wearing spectacles of contempt. You don't know how I feel when you neglect me; you only care about yourself and your desires!" I shouted from behind.

By then, Ashima's dad had stood from his seat and reached Papa, requesting him to relax and have his dinner. But Papa was in no mood to listen. He took steps back, shouting, "I am neglecting you? You left us alone and moved out for the choice of life you wanted. You never cared about our feelings. You were the only concern for yourself and your wife, Ashima. Now when you are planning a baby, you need your mother, you called her. Before that, in the last two years, did you ever call her to your place?

"I was afraid of you and your reacrion, so was not calling you both. Try to understand, Papa."

"Leave it na, please let it go," Mummy told Papa.

"I would have never entered your home if your mother had not forced me to," Papa replied coming closer to me. I raised my voice for the first time in front of him and then tears filled my eyes. I was pushing my heart a lot to stop the tears and not let others know my weakness. But I wanted my heart to pour its feelings that day. And I again replied with a heavy voice this time, "You came because you wanted Ashima to worry. You lost your son, and so you want me to lose my baby."

I looked straight into his eyes. His face was not clear to me due to my tears, but I know he was staring at me with anger. And then he slapped me hard on my left cheek. The slap was as loud as a clap and stung my face. I staggered backwards, clutching my face, my eyes watering. Silence filled the room. I kept holding the dining table chair, with my head down.

And then, I took a step towards Papa and again tried to look into his eyes and replied, "Every night, me and Ashima have been making greeting cards for you, thinking you would start loving us, but we were wrong. This girl whom you hate, loves you like crazy, but she is wrong. This girl who knew you hate me, but still wanted me to love you, she is wrong. But Ashima, today I won. I was correct. He never loved me and he will never love us."

I replied in a thick, soft voice and turned to leave the house, picking the car keys.

"Where are you going Kartik? Wait!" Ashima shouted from behind. But I didn't respond to her too. She came taking long steps to the balcony and leaned to check on me. I looked up and found her standing there; she called me again. "Teddy, wait! Where are you going?"

My eyes were filled with tears, and I did not want Ashima to see them. It was her sixth month and I didn't want her to worry. I opened the door of the car and was about to get in, when Ashima again called, "Teddy, please don't go."

Hearing her soft voice, I wanted to stop, but I wanted to run away from the situation for some time. Without replying to her, I sat in the car and drove away. I didn't want to talk to her as well, as she hadn't listened to me and invited them in the first place. I tried to run away from them all. I wanted to be alone and cry out loud.

I drove my car towards Greater Noida Expressway, a place where I loved to be alone and watch stars. I could feel the emptiness in my heart, even when I had the most lovely person, my Ashima in my life. I wanted things to be perfect, but life is not so easy. I kept driving fast, letting my tears flow. I never smoke, but that day I bought a packet of cigarettes. I tried to burn my emotions, my tears, my feelings and let everything go away in its smoke. As I placed my hands in my pocket to pull out money to pay, I realized I had left my mobile behind. I was worried Ashima might be trying to call me, though I did not want to talk to anyone at that moment.

Sometimes I felt I had made a mistake by only loving her and leaving everything behind, but when I saw her, I realized I had done the right thing. I could not have been so happy without her. When I think of my father, I feel, yes, I had not lived up to his aspirations, but his perception to blame Ashima was not correct. She always tried to patch up things and never wanted us to be apart. It's just the turns in life which presented them in such a way. I drove my car at a speed above hundred kilometers per hour and reached my favourite spot. I parked my car and stepped out, pulling out a cigarette.

After placing the cigarette on my lips, I tried lighting it with a matchstick. I found it tough to burn as I was never a smoker. It took me three to four tries to finally light it. I took my first puff, and then the second, and so on. My tears had dried by then, but not the emotions and feelings. Whenever I tried to think about Papa, my tears started to roll down my cheeks. With every puff, I could remember my childhood days, when Papa used to drop me to school, play with me, help me cover my books, help me with my homework and would kiss me on my forehead every morning before I went to school. I started smoking the cigarettes one after the other. I wanted to think about something else, but don't know why my mind retook me to my memories of the time spent with him, making me cry over and over.

As much as I tried to hold it, the pain came out like an uproar from my throat in the form of a silent scream. The beads of salty water started falling one after another, without any sign of stopping. I hit the car door and tried to scream, but the sound of the passing cars drowned my voice. The world turned into a blur, and so did all the sounds.

Almost an hour passed and I kept sitting on my car bonnet. I continued smoking. I didn't know what happened at home after I left. I was worried about Ashima, but decided to go back after a while. I wanted to let my tears dry off completely.

9

Letter from my father

*I am writing this letter, because I know I am one of the worst
fathers. My love turned out to be the villain in my son's life.
I didn't know when all this happened, but I lost my best friend,
my son, and this was something which had a tremendous impact
on both of us.*

*You'll be thinking, I am a fool. So what if my son fell in love,
so what if he married a girl whom he loved, so what if he didn't
become an engineer? But what to do about feelings and emotions
which do not understand, when understanding is needed the most.*

*I remember the day Kartik was born. He became my reason
to live. I love my wife a lot, but not more then Kartik. You can
call me a possessive father, but yes, it was true. I wanted my son
to be my shadow. I wanted everyone in this world to know him
and know me as his father.*

Yes, I am selfish because I wanted myself to be known as his father and that was not my only desire. I wanted to live with him forever. I wanted him to take care of me when I got old. And what was my mistake? Every parent has desires from their children, and so did I.

He loved Ashima, and I noticed the same on the day when we met Ashima the first time in school with him. Kartik's body language, his eyes, his voice reflected how much he loved her. I was never against his choice, or I must say, I was proud of his decision. I remember that day, I came home and congratulated my wife, saying that our son had grown up.

He cycled outside her society every evening; it was not something I didn't know, but being a father, I wanted him to enjoy his teenage years, though without getting his studies or his aim affected. He was doing very well in his studies, and so I never had any objection. For me, I was the most successful father. My son was studying well; he had a beautiful and intelligent girlfriend; everything was well placed and settled. But then Kartik made a mistake by taking Arts. It's not that I wanted to oppose his wish, but I knew how much he loved maths and engineering. Just that I never understood that he loved Ashima more than both of them. I got blind and could not see his love for her.

That night, at the time of dinner, I didn't want to create a scene in front of his in-laws, but I got annoyed finding Kartik not eating non-veg food, which once used to be his favourite. For me, it was the influence of Ashima and his in-laws, and that was something that irked me. I thought he would support me, but he stood his ground. In fact, it was the first time he raised his voice against me. I wanted to cry, but controlled myself as didn't want to seem weak in front of others. He walked out in anger, which he had never done before. I wanted to stop him, but my ego restrained me.

After Kartik left, it was the first time that Ashima spoke openly to me, and still with respect and love. I respect her for that. She told me how much Kartik loved me, she told me about the greeting cards which they had made daily and left on the bench. She explained the efforts he was making to come closer to me. I broke down hearing her words. I had not been neglecting his efforts to reach me, but I was growing old and recently had my cataract operation. Kartik may not know, but I can't read clearly now. That was the reason I ignored all the cards on the bench. I threw them all, thinking they were waste paper. I am not a heartless father, who would not hug my child who was calling out to me with his words.

I could see tears in Ashima's eyes, while she was telling me the love she and Kartik had for me and indeed got reflected in them. I could not let my tears stop hearing her and felt ashamed of my deeds. I asked Ashima to call him and let me talk to him, but he was not carrying his cell phone. I understood the love and understanding they both had for each other when Ashima informed me that Kartik would be at Greater Noida Expressway. She correctly knew when he wanted to be alone.

Ashima was happy as I hugged her. I wanted my family to be complete and asked Ashima for the location. I also apologized to her parents. She could not travel along with me as the doctor had suggested rest, but she explained to me precisely the point where I could find Kartik. Rohit, her brother, joined me as we drove to the Greater Noida Expressway.

I am a bad father, I never meant to be. I wonder if it's just what happens when you take a love that strong and mix it up with ambition and fear. Like every decision ever made, they got based on the combination of the facts at hand and the personality involved. My ambition overtook my love and resulted in a sour relationship. I moved to make things correct. I decided to hug him and say sorry to him.

While Rohit was driving, I pulled out a tissue paper from the car dash and scribbled a greeting card for Kartik. I drew a man holding the hand of his son and wrote above it,

'There was a time when I showed you the way, but thanks to you for showing me the correct path, my son. I am sorry for all my mistakes. Love you, your Papa.

Kartik's Papa'

10

My tears dried off after five cigarettes while I sat lost in thoughts on the car bonnet. I was looking at the cars passing by and was humming, *'Everything I do, I would do it for you,'* when I heard a car stop at some distance from me. I turned to check; it was Papa's car driven by Rohit. I understood, it was Ashima who had explained to them the location. I got down from the bonnet.

Papa stepped out opening the door, with his face down to avoid eye contact. Rohit shouted to reach me, "Kartik, Papaji wants to talk to you."

Without replying, I turned my face to the other side.

"At least listen to him once, please Kartik," he tried to convince me.

I was angry with Papa, whom I loved the most. But I was his son and wanted to remain angry now. I didn't reply, nor turned towards him, but yes, I pulled out the cigarette packet from my pocket and threw it on the side, hiding it from him.

For a few seconds, there was no sound, except the noise of moving vehicles, and then Rohit patted on my back. "Papaji has given this for you."

I took the tissue paper he handed me with brooding eyes. A smile and tears appeared together as I read what he had written. That was the perfect gift I had received in many years. It would not be wrong to say, I had missed his love, laughter and scolding for many years. And now it was time to hug him tight and say sorry for all the wrongs I did.

With teary eyes and a smile on my face, I turned towards him to find him spreading his arms to hug me. I had waited for this day for seven long years. I was waiting for this day since I was a boy. I was waiting for this since I became a man. Without wasting a second more, I took long steps to reach him, just when unknowingly, a speeding car took the wrong lane and went across the side grass lawn.

I saw it, and at the last second, I jumped. My body hit the hood of the car, and I screamed. My bones, muscles and joints, and organs felt like they were being smashed into a tiny box. My lungs contracted with such force that I was afraid they would fold into themselves. My torso and head smashed against the tar road while my arms and legs were flailing, searching for somewhere to hold and stop the forward movement my body was thrown with. The only sound that filled my ears was the crushing of glass mixed with the sharp crackles of my bones. Then suddenly, everything became light. I was flying through the air, my broken body almost limp from the impact that had occurred nanoseconds before. I could taste the coppery blood pooling in my mouth. I could feel it grazing my teeth and soaking my tongue. I felt the aches and cracks in my bones. Each crack felt as though rocks were burrowing into my skin.

And then, everything went silent. I was dragged to some distance and when I finally stopped, I tried to pull myself up to run towards Papa. I was happy as nothing had happened to me. I was not in pain – with no bruises, no fractures. Nothing.

And then I saw Papa, sitting on the tar road, crying loudly. He was covered with blood. On his body, his shirt, his hands. He was holding my body that lay in a pool of blood. I was scared, seeing myself in a pool of blood. For sometime, I could not understand what had happened to me. How could I see myself lying there? Was I dead or I was dreaming? What was going on? No, I could not die so suddenly, I was about to hug my Papa. I was a son going to be a proud father. I wanted to live my life with Ashima. Oh, god! Can you listen to me? I could not die in such a way. I wanted to live. I tried to cry, but no tears were flowing from my eyes. I was weeping, but no one was able to hear me. I called Papa. I shouted at Rohit, but no one could see me, no one was listening to me, no was hearing my pain which was more significant than the bruises on my body.

"Listen, Papa. Please talk to me. I want to live, Papa!"

"Hey! Rohit, please do something. I am here, I am still here. Please take me home, brother."

I was pleading. I was shouting. I was touching my soul. I was trying to feel my body. I was trying to touch my Papa, but everything just failed. I looked helpless. I could see everything, I could feel everything, but no one was able to feel me.

Rohit and a few passersby came and helped my father who was holding my body. Rohit, without wasting time, placed me in the back seat of the car with the help of a few people. Papa was still holding my head in his lap, crying.

"Open your eyes beta, talk to me." Papa was rubbing my forehead and was crying aloud. His hands were covered in my blood, as he was trying to stop the blood from flowing out of my body. I wanted to console him, knowing the fact that he could not listen to me anymore.

"Rohit, drive fast to the nearest hospital. He is not speaking. I will never forgive myself if something happens to him. Open your eyes, Kartik, *mera bachcha*, open your eyes."

His tears were dripping on my face, and I could feel his pain. I was waiting for this day for years. To be on his lap and get his love, and today, when he was with me, I could not even feel his touch, his warmth. I felt frustrated about what had happened. I wanted to bang my hands on the car dashboard, which I was not able to do. I tried to shout, but my voice was stuck within myself.

"Uncle, please control yourself, everything will be fine. We'll reach in a few minutes," Rohit replied to Papa and drove to JP Hospital which was the closest. Rohit called the hospital emergency and asked them to be ready with a stretcher at the gate.

I still believed it was a nightmare which would get over as soon as the doctors would cure me. The hospital boys immediately took my body on the stretcher and rushed to the operation theater. My father was running behind as fast as his aging legs could take him, without bothering about his clothes which were covered with blood and mud. I was worried about him; he was a person who loved cleanliness and could never bear even a stain on his shirt.

Rohit asked Papa to sit outside the operation theater, and he went to the side to call up the others. I went with him and heard when he said, "Papa, please do not react to what I am telling you. You need to be calm. Ashima must not get affected by what I am going to say."

He continued after hearing something from the other side, "Kartik met with a terrible accident. We've brought him to JP Hospital. Please come along with the others, but do not panic, as it may affect Ashima's baby."

He placed his phone back and rushed to Papa, who was crying.

Disclaimer: If you are too emotional, stop reading this story now. If you're wondering how a ghost ended up writing, then my friend, you must know that love knows no barriers.

Papa was sitting on the steel chairs placed at the corner with his hands on the side rest, pressing his face with his palm, trying to stop his tears. I stood at some distance and cursed the circumstances. I wanted to turn back time. The doctor came out opening the door of the operation theater. It was a surprise to see Sanjeev there, my batch-mate from my school in Chakrata. He walked straight to my Papa and said something placing his hands on his shoulder, as Papa stood with folded hands to plead.

Then, Papa cried as if his brain had got shredded from the inside. Emotional pain flowed out of every pore of his body. From his mouth came a cry so raw that even the eyes of the strangers around us were suddenly wet with tears. Rohit tried to grab my father so that his violent shaking would not cause him to fall. His whole world had crumbled; now there was only pain to break him, pain sufficient to change him beyond recognition.

Sometimes some exceptions change everyone's lives in one shot. I rushed into the operation theater and saw my body lying on the table. The nurse was trying to clean blood on my face – the blood over my still eyes and vacant face. Am I dead? I could not understand what had happened in just a few hours. My life with my love Ashima and our expected baby, had just shattered.

As I turned, I saw Papa entering the operation theater with Rohit, who was holding Papa firmly, wiping his tears. Papa reached my body with slow steps, sobbing, and then stood by my side.

He slowly moved his hands and touched my still hand, bursting into sobs. It started slow and gentle, but it rose to a wail that tore my heart. He then came close to my face and cursed softly, stroking my forehead saying, *"Beta,* don't do this to me. Please get up again and hug me. What will I say to Ashima? I told her I am leaving to bring you back, and that we will live happily ever after." He wiped his tears and then sat next to me firmly and continued, "Okay, see I am not crying now. You remember when you were younger, I used to tell you a story every morning before school? You'd keep closing your eyes till the story ended and then would jump to hug me saying, you had fooled me. Let me tell you a story today."

Rohit tried to interrupt him, but Papa stopped him saying he must not disturb him while he was narrating the story.

"Once, Kartik asked his mother, why people at the bottom of the earth do not fall into space. Mom got confused and wondered how to answer her baby Kartik." Papa was careless about his tears flowing from his eyes as he continued.

"But Papa was sitting by her side and replied, because everyone is pulled to the earth as she is our mother and a mother never leaves her child alone." Papa stopped, he could not speak further. He kept looking at the wall and then continued sobbing, "You will miss your school bus Kartik, time to jump on me, time to say, 'Papa, I love you'. Get up beta, please get up." And he broke down. He almost lost his balance and was about to fall to the floor. I rushed to hold him, but failed. Thanks to Rohit for holding him.

I felt helpless, unable to do anything about what was going on. I wanted to shout and bang my head on the wall, but I could not even do that. I could not see my Papa breaking down and went outside the room. I heard that in life after death, there will be a foggy road on which one needs to walk to meet god. But I could not see any foggy road then. I could not find god anywhere. Will I continue to be like a ghost forever? I was trying to solve my confusion when I saw Ashima along with her parents walking down the corridor. She was searching for me, and it seemed like she was still not aware of my death. Her eyes were searching for me, and I ran to hug her. I tried to hug her again and again, but I couldn't. I was shouting, but no one could listen, *"I love you Ashima, I love you."*

From the other end entered Sanjeev and came walking fast to her. "Hey, Ashima," he called her from behind.

Ashima turned to check and recognized him with a pause, "Hey, Sanjeev, if I am not mistaken. You are a doctor now, wow! Amazing."

Sanjeev understood she was still not aware of my demise and hugged her politely.

"I am looking for Kartik. You remember Kartik na, our classmate. He is my husband now, and see, I am carrying his baby. We will be proud parents soon. He met with a small accident, I was told. I am not sure where is he. Do you know?" she questioned him with a smile.

Sanjeev looked pained, and before he could say anything, Rohit came and without uttering a word, hugged Ashima.

"What happened, Bhai? Why are you hugging me? Is everything fine? Where is Teddy?" Hearing Ashima's words, Rohit broke down crying loudly as if his heart had broken. He kept hugging her and replied, "We've lost him, sister. We've lost him."

Ashima immediately pushed him, "What are you saying Bhai? No, it's not possible. He is very naughty, you don't know him. He always plays pranks on me."

Rohit was silent, still sobbing. He placed his hands on her cheeks to explain with his eyes.

"I don't believe you; he can't do this. Teddy told me he will be with me my entire life and will kiss me in front of our babies' children. Where is he? Tell me. I want to meet him." Ashima looked relaxed as if everyone was joking. She didn't understand, or pretended not to understand. Her eyes were still not wet, and she looked normal. Her parents broke down hearing Rohit's words.

"Sanjeev, listen to what Bhai is saying. He is such a fool. Bhai, meet Sanjeev. He is my friend from Dehradun and a doctor. He will get Teddy fit and fine."

She turned to her mom saying, "Mummy, please don't get fooled by Kartik's pranks; he is such a naughty guy."

Sanjeev took hold of her hand and asked her to follow him. By that time, my body had been shifted to a room next to the operation theater, and Papa was still sitting next to me. Ashima's feet slowed down. Her breath could be heard in the silence of cries. She strolled along, holding Sanjeev's hand. Looking at her coming, Papa stood up to cry and tried to hug her. But she slightly pushed him with her left side, ignoring him and continued staring, her eyes unblinking on my body wrapped in a white cloth placed at some distance. She kept walking and smiled at Sanjeev and Rohit as if they all were lying to her. She still believed it was a prank. But her smile had a fear of death and loneliness, which she never had imagined.

She reached my body while Sanjeev removed the cloth from my face. I was dead. Ashima crouched, one hand over my still chest. She picked up my hand, cold and pale, touched it to her distended stomach, closing her eyes for just a moment. In that eternal second, she felt my presence like the last kiss which we never got to have. Her mind struggled to stay in that moment, to keep me close.

She was still not crying, but had become rigid. Everyone looked at her strange behaviour in shock. She then came close to my face and kissed me softly on my lips. I could not feel her touch and wanted to kiss her again. She then brought her two fingers in front of my closed eyes, "Hey Teddy, pick one."

She paused and waited for me to pick. I walked towards her and tried to choose one, still crying without tears.

"*Mera baccha, mera* Teddy, pick one finger na. I know it's annoying, but you know I love this," she again asked my dead body.

"Bhai, ask him to pick one finger."

She asked Rohit and then answered herself, "Leave it, today he is angry, else he would choose one finger."

She then stood and pushed my body to the right side. Finding her doing so, Sanjeev tried to help her. "Thanks, Sanjeev, you are such a nice friend," she replied and tried to adjust herself next to me on the bed. Looking at her, everyone in the room broke and cried, but she got lost in her way of handling the situation. She slept next to my dead body, placing her head on my shoulder, which she always loved, and put her left hand on my chest.

"Would you like to talk to me, Teddy?" she questioned my body innocently. Hearing her, my mother, who was crying loud, sat on the floor, shedding tears. But Ashima was lost in herself and continued, "Why are you not hugging me tight? Teddy, I am feeling so sleepy, and you know, I can't sleep without hugging you. *Meri Mandaakini, chal* hug me na."

She closed her eyes and hugged me. "You know, today our baby kicked me fifteen times. He is excited about coming out and playing with you. We will play chess with him like we used to play during our school summer breaks. You remember, Teddy?"

Sanjeev, who was observing all this from a distance, could not control his tears, and went to Rohit and asked him to take Ashima away from my body, to avoid any infection during her pregnancy. Hearing him, Rohit turned towards the bed and softly put his hands on Ashima's forehead. "Sister, why don't you let Kartik sleep for sometime? He got hurt na, so he is resting.

Let's go home. He will come back soon," Rohit tried to convince her and helped her to stand up.

"But why is he sleeping? Why is he not talking to me, Bhai?"

"He will talk, I will bring him back to home," Rohit assured her.

Hearing him, she stood and moved to the side of the room and stood politely, still not crying. She looked at everyone and then proceeded to my mother, who was wailing at the corner.

"Mamma, what happened? Why are you crying? Teddy is fine; he is just sleeping due to the medicines. Stop crying." Ashima hugged my mummy and tried to console her.

"Na beta, our Kartik has gone, he will not wake up now…" my mummy yelled amidst her sobs.

"Sanjeev, you explain to her," Ashima replied and again stood in the corner. She was in profound shock seeing me dead, and I was afraid for our baby. I moved to her and stood in front of her, facing her. She was looking towards the wall, unblinking.

I kept looking into her eyes and said calmly, "Angel, my love. I know you cannot hear me, but I am sure our hearts can talk. I may not be with you physically anymore, but my soul will be with you forever. I am not sure why this happened, but I know, I lived for you and will continue to be with you. You are my only Angel to take me to heaven; else everything is a myth. I am always here with you. I took birth to love you, and I knew that since I met you. Your smile is my energy tonic and your eyes my breath. Please do not neglect me or forget me, as I will be with you and for you, because I love you." I said and heard a loud cry as the ward boy covered my face and body with a white cloth. Rohit was signing some documents to get my body released.

"I have arranged for an ambulance to drop Kartik's body to your home," Sanjeev informed Rohit.

Ashima was still silent, smiling and talking to everyone as if nothing had happened. She tried to move to everyone and kept consoling them until the ambulance was arranged. Rohit preferred to take Ashima and the other females in the car, while both the fathers decided to go with my body in the ambulance. I chose to be with Ashima.

Rohit started driving, while Ashima was in the front seat. Ashima's mom was trying to make my mummy relax and just after a few minutes of the drive, Ashima started to laugh. She was blushing and wanted to say something.

"You know Bhai, what happened last night? My baby started kicking a lot, and Kartik just went mad feeling it. The whole night, he just kept waiting for the kicks. And then he removed all his clothes, and just wearing his shorts, he performed the 'towel dance' like Salman." She again laughed and then pulled her mobile and continued, "Wait, let me show you. I recorded it."

She turned her mobile and flashed a video, where I was dancing with a towel *'Jeene ke hain chaar din, baaki hain bekaar din…'* She started laughing out loud watching it, leaving tears in everyone's eyes. She was enjoying it a lot, playing that video again and again. I could feel Rohit getting annoyed in pain, and after sometime, he applied the car brakes, shouting at my Angel, "Why you do not understand? Our Kartik has gone, he is no more. He has left us."

There was an eerie silence. Ashima slapped him hard, "*Ye mat soch* that because you are elder to me, I cannot hit you. I am your same wrestler sister and can slap you anytime, especially if you talk rubbish," she replied, referring to their childhood game.

Till now, it was Rohit who was acting strong and keeping everything in control, but then he too broke down like a baby. He started sobbing, letting his tears drip on the car seat. Ashima hugged him immediately, saying, *"Oh mera pyara Bhai,* sorry I slapped you. You are still crying like a small kid." She kissed him on his cheek to let him sob. Rohit continued crying, but started the car and drove on.

That night was the most terrible night for my family. My body was placed at the center of the hall after removing all the furniture, and the cremation was planned for the morning. To handle Ashima was not an easy task the whole night. At times she tried to lie down next to my body, hugging me, and sometimes she prepared a cup of tea for me, saying to everyone that Kartik liked to have tea in the night with Parle G biscuits.

I placed myself next to my cold and pale body, observing everyone sobbing and talking about me. I was afraid about the next morning when my body would get burnt to ashes. Would I get the sensation of burning? Would I feel the pain? Would I move to heaven after the cremation? My soul was already in pain seeing everyone in tears, and the next morning, I was not sure how I would handle the pain.

The night passed, and with the morning sunlight, I was given a bath and dressed in my best for the ride to the next world. I stood next to my body and walked into my bedroom to find Ashima. She was looking fresh, sitting with folded legs on the bed, doing her yoga. I moved and sat in front of her, to observe her closed eyes and take her glimpse forever in my soul.

I wanted to tell her about everything which I had not told her in those nine years, and then I started with a husky voice, "You are my world, which is everywhere in this space. I loved to walk with you, to touch your fingers while walking. I loved to sing with you, to see you laughing at my lousy rhythm. I loved to dance with you, to touch your waist. I loved to sleep next to you, only to wake up with you. I loved to hug you, to hear the sound of your heart. I loved to smile with you, to assure I was with you.

"Today I am next to you, but very far away. Today I cannot hug you, but feel the hugs which we gave each other many times in these nine years. Today I cannot smile at you, but will smile remembering all the laughs we had. Today I cannot touch you, but will still walk with you to feel the touch we once shared." I paused in pain and kept looking at her when a crying sound came from the hall. I stood and moved outside and so did Ashima, taking small steps.

My body was being lifted, ready to be taken for cremation, and everyone was crying aloud. Ashima was quiet – standing at the corner with no words, no smile – no reactions at all. Just the silence of love that she was feeling. Every other eye was in tears, and as my body reached the door, Ashima shouted with a loud cry.

"Teddy. Stop, Teddy. Do not leave me alone, Teddy." And she burst into tears, which she had kept holding since the night. I always said Ashima loved like a hurricane. I was right. When she started, she cried with more violence than any gale. Not to have me right there was torture to her soul. She rushed to my body and pulled everyone back, holding my body to make them place my body back. Her father allowed it, as he wanted her to break out, to let her emotions turn into tears. I tried to hold her and say that I was with her and would always love her.

She came down on her keens, without considering that she was pregnant and hugged my cold body. She then cupped my cheeks with both her hands. She wiped her face on her shoulder, turning her face to the left, then came close to my face to speak softly with a heavy voice full of tears, "Teddy, don't do this to me *bachcha*. Please get up baby. You were there with me for the last nine years. You are my habit, my need. I cannot live without you. I would have died along if our baby was not within me. Why are you doing this, Teddy? You promised you will always be with me; you promised we would celebrate our fiftieth anniversary; you promised you would hug me when we get old; you promised you would kiss me till we don't have teeth in our mouth. What happened to all those promises?"

Still crying, she placed her face on my chest. Mummy tried to console her and pull her away, but she was not in agreement to leave me and started speaking again, "You know na, Teddy, I am weak in maths, who will do the calculation for daily needs? You know I need bed tea, who will make it for me? You know I cannot handle kids, who will help me manage our baby? Speak up Teddy, speak up, please. Teddy, please. I close my eyes to sleep because you used to be by my side. What the hell will I do without you, Teddy?" Now she shouted with a cry. Her tears were rolling like a floodgate that had finally opened.

Rohit and the others started raising my body again to take me away from her. She kept on crying, holding the white cloth. I too started shouting, "Stop, do not take me. I want to be with my Angel, please do not take me. God help me, let me go back to my love…"

But no one was there to listen to me and my pain. My body got taken down the very stairs using which I left for my office every day kissing Ashima at the door. But that day I was running behind my body, leaving my love in tears. I reached downstairs to the road. With pained eyes, I looked up and saw my Angel standing, with tears in her eyes, sobbing uncontrollably, waving at me to say goodbye forever and ever.

Standing below in the crowd, among the hue and cry, I could hear what Ashima was murmuring standing at the corner of the balcony looking at my body for the last time.

"You've gone, and this time for so long. I still don't believe that this is the end. You know, it is so hard to see a person that you used to love going to another world. It is so hard for me to turn and not see you behind me. I wish that you were here, so I could tell you things I can't tell you again; tell you that I love you, tell you that I'll never forget you, tell you that I'll always see you in the stars at night, tell you that I will miss you."

And the next drop of her tears landed on the floor of the balcony.

11

A week passed by and life for everyone stood still. I could not find any change in my soul and continued to be with Ashima all the time. I was in deep pain finding her crying all night, all alone. She started sleeping with the lights switched on and grabbed a pillow, to overcome my absence. Papa was silent most of the time, and cried when he was alone, while mummy was trying to cheer up the others as she knew it was a tough time for Ashima and her family.

It was so early to determine where Ashima would stay, but till the completion of many official formalities, she preferred to stay back in the same flat. I could feel the depth of silence in her life. Since my death, Ashima had stopped talking to Papa, as if she believed him to be responsible for my death. She was depressed and silent. She preferred being alone, not at all concerned about her looks. She did not even remember when she had taken a bath last time or combed her hair.

It was eleven in the night, Ashima was in the kitchen filling up a bottle of water for the night. She looked lost as if she had no one to talk to in her life. The same home which was a house full of chatter and laughter for both of us was now submerged in a lake of silence. Ashima picked up her bottle and walked with controlled steps to her room. I was following her like a shadow, and then she stopped, as if she felt me, and turned behind with curious eyes looking all around. She then switched off the lights of the living room and went to our bedroom. She placed the bottle on the side table, on the one I used to sit and write letters for our baby and positioned herself on the bed.

"I am not sure, but I feel Teddy, you are always with me," she spoke softly, dropping a single drop of tear. I nodded listening to her as if she could feel my response. She kept silent for some more time, unblinking, looking at the ceiling, with her hands on her stomach. "Baby, would you like to see pictures of your papa?" she asked innocently caressing our baby and then stood to pull out our wedding album from the drawer below the study desk.

Our marriage album was on the lowest shelf. She tried adjusting her stomach and then gently pulled the album. She then went to her bed, placed a pillow at the back and sat taking a long breath. I always loved her hands with her nails painted in pretty colours, but that day I was sad looking at her fingers sans nail paint. I may not be in her life, but she must continue to do what I loved, I thought. Looking at her, I was wondering at the futility of so many rituals to be followed after a loved one's demise. Being a soul, I would be happier and relaxed after death if Ashima would be laughing, wearing the same colourful clothes as she used to dress in or wear the same colourful bangles which looked beautiful on her hands. I know she was missing all those things and I was in greater pain finding these changes in her appearance.

She opened the photo album with wet eyes and caressed the first picture in which I was smiling at her, and she was laughing at me, relaxed and feeling loved. Looking at the picture, she smiled like a baby, and then one warm drop of tear started rolling down her soft white cheeks.

"See your Papa, looking so cute. You know what he was saying to me that I laughed?" she asked talking to our baby and replied, "He told me coming close to my ears, that *I* have grown up so fast, he still imagines me to be in school, and me fantasizing about our wedding night." Ashima took a pause, went silent and then with the wan look she continued, "Your papa was very naughty. I wish you could have enjoyed with him."

She kept turning pages one after the other, telling our story to our baby and letting me feel nostalgic about the time we spent before our marriage. I moved to her side and started thinking about that day when I got a job and rushed to her home in Greater Noida with an Amul Butterscotch ice cream pack.

"Aunty, where is Ashima?" I asked in excitement as she opened the door.

"She is in her room. What happened? Why are you in such a rush?" Aunty questioned from behind as I rushed upstairs to her room.

"Aunty, now be ready. I am soon going to call you mummy," I replied to her. Ashima's parents knew about our relationship, and they had already accepted me as their son-in-law. Aunty laughed as I rushed to her room.

"Angel, open the damn door," I knocked as it was locked from inside. I could hear her shouting from inside to wait. But

I was getting impatient as I had news for her. "What the hell are you doing, Angel? Open the door." I managed to bang on it again, before she finally opened it.

"What happened Teddy? I was changing," she replied moving back inside the room. I immediately pulled her catching her wrist, bringing her closer to me, and almost hugged her.

"Are you a fool? What are you doing Teddy? I am at home. Mom can come in any time."

"Let her come. I am not afraid of her anymore," I replied with a naughty smile.

"What happened? You are fearless today," she questioned giving me a quizzical expression.

"Guess?"

"Don't tell me; you got selected for the interview you went for today?" She questioned giving a radiant smile. She always knew everything about me – my smiles, my fear, my love.

I took a step back and brought the ice cream pack to the front. She looked at it slack-jawed and jumped to hug me, tightly, very tight and kissed me on my lips. "I love you, Teddy. I love you."

"What happened? Why are you both making so much noise?" Ashima's mom called from downstairs.

Hearing her, Ashima gave a mischievous look and shut the door.

"I am so happy for you Teddy," she replied with a big fat smile on her face, and I immediately interrupted, "Not for me, I am happy for us."

She nodded smiling, and hugged me again.

"And now it's time for your favourite ice cream, baby," I replied with eyes wide open.

And she replied, "And I'm eating it all today."

I opened the wrapper and found the spoons missing. "Hey Angel, go get two spoons from the kitchen."

She stood and was about to open the door, but then stopped. "What happened, go get na," I asked her.

She turned back and started unwrapping the ice cream pack. "What are you doing?" I questioned her with confused looks, as she put her fingers into the ice cream pack.

She pulled some ice cream with her hands and placed it in my mouth, "Teddy, today I promise I will love you forever. Today I promise I will be there for you and with you. Eating ice cream with fingers, for me, is the new way to get married, and today I am getting married to you." It was a sudden reaction. And this was always her habit – to surprise me with her actions.

She then went down on her knees and pulled some more ice cream with her fingers, and with her eyes staring into mine, she said, "Will you marry me, Teddy? Today, now, at this moment?"

Hearing her, I could only feel the truth in her words and without speaking a single word, I held her hand and took it to my mouth with love. She had asked me my desire for which I was waiting since a long time. I looked here and there, and then pulled a chair and placed the ice cream pack on it.

Our marriage had been inevitable from the time we were teens. We were inseparable. We both were the centre of the universe for the other. We both were so relaxed in each other's company, so caring. For years, we remained devoted to one other. Through ups and downs, we supported one another. Being with her, being her husband was something which I always believed in. Only the social tag of marriage was needed.

I made her stand, holding her hands and started taking a circle of the ice cream pack. "You wanted to marry today, now, at this moment. Here I am, for you, forever and ever."

Ashima looked at me with love and a smile of satisfaction when I leaned on my knees and asked her if she was ready to take the seven vows with me then and there. She nodded with a smile and tears in her eyes.

I started walking holding her hand saying, "I will keep you happy and will offer you all the best amenities in life."

Ashima replied, taking a circle, "I will take care of our home, and all household. I promise I will make our house a home and will be the best homemaker for you."

We both stopped after completing the first vow and let each other have a bite of ice cream with our hands. I smiled and started the second vow.

"Together we will protect our house and children."

Ashima replied in return, "I will be by your side as your courage and strength. I will rejoice in your happiness. In return, you will love me solely."

I took a pause, turned and replied giving a mischievous look, "Really, I cannot love anyone else then?" She slapped me playfully and put some ice cream into my mouth. And so did I.

It was time for the third vow, and I continued saying, "I will work to grow wealthy and prosperous for you, our children and our family."

Ashima looked into my eyes, as I turned to her saying, "I will love you solely for the rest of my life, as you are my husband. Every other man in my life will be secondary."

We continued taking helpings of ice cream, "You have brought sacredness in my life and have completed me. I promise to respect you and your feelings."

Ashima replied with attitude, "I will shower you with love and joy in our life. I will keep you happy in every way I can."

For us, our vows were our marriage and our love was our blessing. We were as serious as we'd be in an actual wedding.

I continued taking the fifth vow holding her hand, "You are my best friend and will be my best friend forever. I would only pray to god to bless you forever."

Ashima was lost in my love, and so was I. She was nodding at my words and then replied, "Your happiness is my happiness, and your sorrow is my sorrow. I will trust and honour you and will strive to fulfill all your wishes."

I stopped and took some ice cream in my hand and placed it in her mouth, but my hands were slow now and wanted to keep touching her. She kept looking into my eyes and made me take a bite. In our ice cream marriage of love, we could not feel that ice cream had started melting and was flowing on the floor. Without noticing it, we started for our sixth vow, "Today I am the happiest person, as I have you, whom I dreamt of having as my wife for seven long years. Today we completed six steps together; I want you to walk with me for my whole life and make me the happiest person on this earth."

I took a vow waiting for Ashima to reply, "I will always be by your side and will walk hand in hand in pleasure and sorrow."

By now, the ice cream was all over our faces and lips, but we were lost in love. We were at the final step of the vow, and I wanted to ask her again before taking the last step.

"Angel, are you ready for the last vow? If any doubt, you can stop me, because for me these ice cream vows were not fun, for me you are already my wife now."

Ashima kept looking at me. I could see tears of happiness in her eyes and then she moved in front of me, took hold of my hand

and started to walk saying, "As god is a witness, I am now your wife. We will love, honour and cherish each other forever."

I was feeling love in every corner of the room. I replied to her, "We are now husband and wife, and are one. You are mine, and I am yours for eternity."

I dipped my fingers into the ice cream pack for the last time and was about to make her eat it when she stopped me and caught hold of my hand. I gave her a quizzical look. Ashima moved her head closer to me. I stood frozen in both fear and excitement. She leaned in, so her forehead rested against mine. We both closed our eyes, with shaking breaths. "Thank you," she said in barely more than a whisper.

"For what?" I replied, in a low husky voice.

"For being you." Her voice wavered, exhilarated from the love between us.

Ashima gently leaned in and kissed my warm lips. We pulled apart and took shaky, shallow breaths. We were unable to contain ourselves anymore. I held Ashima's head in my hands and pulled her into a fiery and passionate kiss. Her hands worked their way around my body, feeling each line along my perfect physique.

We leaned in for a kiss and started tasting the ice cream through our lips. She let out little whimpers of anticipation. With every bite of each other, we were getting engrossed in the vows which we had just taken. That day, we kissed as husband and wife. That day, our story moved to the next chapter of our life, which had only abundance of happiness in store for us.

On the same day, I called Mummy in Dehradun and informed her about my job. She was pleased and conveyed to me that Papa was also delighted, but Papa didn't talk to me. I told her of my wish to marry Ashima. Mummy knew I loved Ashima, but she never expected me to marry her at the early age of twenty-two. I was immediately called to Dehradun as Papa wanted to meet me. That was the time when everything for me was perfect. Life was going according to plan.

After a week, I took a train to reach Dehradun late evening, and after a formal meeting, we sat for dinner at our dining table. I was expecting the turbulence after my parents learnt of my wish to marry at that age, and that too marry Ashima. The silence was broken with the deep voice of Papa, "It's good you've got a job, congratulations. Now concentrate on your career and do something better in your life."

"Thanks, Papa. I want to talk to you about something," I replied without looking into his eyes.

"I said concentrate on your career, that's all. Government rule says that a boy can marry at twenty-one; it does not mean that you spoil your career for a girl. Which you have already done, by not doing engineering." Papa responded, and his expression showed he didn't want to listen to me at all.

"But I love her, Papa."

"You cannot fill your stomach with love. I am not against you marrying that girl, whatever her name is, but only once you settle down." He was adamant.

I stopped eating and looked rebellious. For me, Ashima was everything and I could not live a day without her. I stood up, leaving my food half-finished and replied, "I disagree. I will be marrying her."

"Why you are here when you have already taken a decision? Could have just sent us an invitation card directly. That girl and her family have you under the spell of black magic, maybe that is why you cannot understand what is right and what is wrong in life," Mummy interrupted.

"Mummy, you too are not supporting me?" I replied turning my face towards Mummy.

"I cannot support every wrong thing you wish for," Mummy replied with a glowering expression.

"You both will never support me. Papa has been behaving weirdly ever since I took arts. Is this how parents behave when children do things according to their wish?" I replied arrogantly.

Papa now stood up from his chair and replied loudly, "You are the biggest fool, and I am ashamed you are my son. Do whatever you want with your life. You are earning; it's your life, do whatever you like. If you invite us to your wedding, we will come as guests. You needn't invite us, in fact." Papa completed and went inside without completing his dinner. Mummy kept looking at me with worried looks and then followed Papa. I didn't cry that day. I was confident about my decision. I picked up my bag and went back to Noida without saying bye to them the same night.

I was lost in old memories when Ashima's sobbing brought me back from the past. It has become a daily ritual to see Ashima sob at night all alone, hugging a pillow, looking at my pictures and videos on her mobile. I was worried for her and our baby. She was just twenty-four, carrying a baby and now was all alone. She stood on the brink of something she couldn't even fathom. The weight of everything seemed to press down on her shoulders, and she struggled to take even a single step forward. My sudden demise was too much, but somehow she kept moving with my memories. The darkness grew darker; the pain became sharper; all of it seemed to only grow in strength, and she began to believe that her life would continue in the same way until her last breath. I was tense and hurt seeing her sad and in pain.

12

One afternoon, Ashima's mother visited our place. She and my mummy sat in the living room, while Ashima was in her bedroom. Since the last few days, Ashima had created a shell around her. She started staying alone silent, lost in herself, thinking about me. Often she would talk to our baby, smile and then start crying.

"Why don't you take Ashima with you for a few days? I am so worried about her," my Mummy suggested.

"You took the words from my mouth. She will also feel better."

Mummy held her hand and replied, "I know we could not give her that love which she deserved in these two years, but I assure you, I and Kartik's Papa both love her a lot."

"I know and understand, but now it's time when we need to handle her and bring her back to normal. She has her whole life in front of her," Ashima's mom replied and stood up to meet her. Her room door was closed. She knocked asking her to open it and then found it was just shut. She entered and found Ashima on her bed with her face to the other side. Her bed was filled with my memories. My pictures, gifts, clothes, watch, everything which I ever used was around her. Her mother was not expecting any less than what she saw. She entered quietly and sat next to her. Ashima didn't show any reaction to her visit, while previously she used to jump in joy.

"Beta, how are you, my Ashima?"

Ashima didn't respond to her question and kept looking away. She had already entered a state of depression. My mummy moved to her side and asked her with a smile, "Ashima beta, see your mummy is here. She wants to take you to her home. Get up and be ready. You will feel better with the change."

Ashima was still silent, with no response.

"Will you come with me, Ashima?" her mom again questioned putting her hand on her forehead.

Her face reflected as if she was not listening to whatever they were saying. My mummy then tried to be a little casual to make her relax and said, "Ashima see what you have done to the room. There's no place to sit on the bed."

And Mummy started adjusting my stuff scattered on the bed.

Ashima shouted as Mummy touched my stuff. "Leave everything, you old lady," she yelled unlike herself.

Mummy immediately dropped the things and moved a step back seeing Ashima aggressive. Her eyes had grown big and red.

"This is my room, my Teddy's room. No one must dare to come inside. He lives with me in this room as he hates you all. Never touch his things!"

Her mom tried to control her, but she was shouting in pain, "I am not going anywhere leaving my Teddy. Leave us alone."

"But beta, try to understand and come to reality," Mummy again tried to persuade her, but she was adamant and shouted back. "Leave the room. Get lost, get lost from our lives!"

She placed her hands on her ears and started shouting as if she didn't want to listen to anyone. Mummy gestured to her mom to leave the room, as her rage would affect her baby. They both left while Ashima continued shouting.

Both of them were in tears finding Ashima is such a condition. They understood she was in severe depression.

"God help my daughter, please help," her mom pleaded. My mummy asked her to take a seat as she brought her a glass of water. Mummy had entered the kitchen when the doorbell rang. She opened the door and found Papa, who had gone to the police station for some formalities as my death had been an accident case.

It was hot outside, and he was sweating. He entered and saw Ashima's mom sitting there. Without saying a word, he greeted her with a namaste from a distance and moved to the kitchen where mummy was pouring out a glass of water. My death had affected two people the most – my Papa and my love Ashima. They both had stopped speaking.

Papa handed over a packet to Mummy. "What is this?"

"What Kartik left in the car. I got it from the police station today. Please hand it over to Ashima, she would remember him." His voice went heavy and was about to cry, but he went to the other room hiding his face. I walked behind him and saw him rushing to sit on the bed and sob. He was crying hard soundlessly. He kept stifling his voice, to show how strong he was, which was not the real case, I knew then. He loved me a lot, I know, but that day I wanted to hug him tight and say, 'Papa, I love you too'.

I left him alone and went to Mummy. She was entering Ashima's room again. She was silent by then and still lost in her thoughts.

"Ashima beta, take this. These are Kartik's things which he was carrying with him on that last day." Mummy placed that packet on the desk and left, without waiting for her response. I remained standing next to her and waited to see her reaction. For the next few minutes, she kept still. And then she bent to pick up the packet. It was a white sealed packet. She turned the polybag upside down to let everything fall out on the desk. Coins, the keys of my car, my purse, some papers and my watch now lay scattered on the table top.

I'd never seen Ashima sit like that – so defeated. Her shoulders shook, her hands hung low, and there was no attempt to conceal or even wipe away her tears. Apart from her reddened face, she was so pale. She sobbed into her hands, and the tears dripped between her fingers, raining down onto the scattered stuff. Her breathing was ragged, gasping, and the strength left her legs. She placed herself back on the bed and picked up my wallet. She started cleaning it as it was covered in mud and blood stains. She then opened it so tenderly, as if she was touching me again. On the left was our picture – Ashima and I smiling and hugging each other. She let her fingers caress it and looked at it for sometime. I placed myself next to her and tried kissing her, though I knew I could not touch her again.

Emotional pain isn't felt the way a cut or bruise is. It is much different, and only the one who has suffered it can tell it is there. Sometimes the pain is at the back of your mind like a pulse. Other times it pushes itself forward demanding attention. Cutting your heart and soul in half, stinging with every breath you take. Ashima's pain was waiting to blow up and come out – a form of her depression.

She closed the wallet and was about to place it to her side when something slipped from it and fell in her lap. With brooding eyes, she picked it and realized it was the key of the wooden box, which I told her that I would hand over to her with the letters to my baby. She brought that key in front of her and cried harder with a smile as if she believed that it was me who had sent that to her. She could not resist herself now, although I had asked her to read these letters when our baby would enter our home. She stood from the bed and started searching for the box, which I had put in the cupboard. I wanted to help her by telling her to look in the closet, yes on the second shelf, last corner, behind the clothes, forgetting that she couldn't hear me anymore. For seconds I forgot I was dead and started interacting with her in excitement, as I now wanted her to read those letters. My messages of love, which only I could complete. My soul will always be in pain as I could not finish all the letters which I planned to write.

She managed to pull out the wooden box, wiping her tears with her left hand. My Angel had grown up suddenly, and I understood it's the twists and turns in our life, which make us wise. She slowly went back to the bed holding the box and picked up the key to open it. She tried unlocking it with her shaky hands. She opened the box and found the things which I had placed in there. Some letters, one dry rose which I had given to her during college, one hand glove, one ribbon which she used to wear in her hair during our school days and lots of my love.

She picked up the rose dolefully and said with a pause, "Baby, you know your Papa gave me this rose in my college, and he had said, 'A single rose can be a garden, and a single you are everything for me.' He had told me the truth indeed."

"Yes, I told the truth, my Angel, because you are the only you in my life. Without you, this Teddy does not exist," I replied hearing her.

She then picked up the hand glove and started telling our baby, "Your Papa loved to trek and once he took me along during our last year of school to the Valley of Flowers. There we exchanged our gloves for fun and look what your Papa did; he kept it all the while."

Next, she pulled out the red ribbon with confused eyes. Then she said excitedly, "Oh my god! This ribbon was with him. I still remember in the class eleventh, I lost my ribbon during lunch time, and I kept looking for it. Finally, I returned home with one braid."

I smiled seeing her smile, but then again, she went silent as she picked up my first letter. The letters placed in a white envelope with the sequence number on top of each one. She checked all of them and then picked up the first envelope – 'My first letter to my baby.' Her expression showed she was building the courage to read it while I kept looking at her.

My dearest Baby,

Hello baby! My love! My darling! I am so excited to be writing this letter.

I am your father, Kartik Verma, but you will know me as Teddy because that is what your mama calls me. So I am your Teddy Papa.

Let me also introduce you to your mother, my wife, my love Ashima, whom I call Angel. And believe me, she is a real angel. You will realize that as you grow up.

You know why I am writing these letters to you, because you are not just a baby, you are a practical form of love, whose theory your mama and I studied for nine long years. Yes, I met your mama when she was just in school and at the first instance, I was in love with her. I can bet you will also fall in love with her when you see her for the first time. My Angel is so beautiful.

We both were so excited knowing that you are coming to our life. Today your mama quit Chinese food for her pregnancy period, which she is crazy about. But I have assured her, that I will take her to a Chinese restaurant daily when she is allowed to. What do you say, you like Chinese food?

Your first month was full of curiosity for both of us. Your mama was feeling nauseous all the time; she could not cook and felt like vomiting. But we both were enjoying the time with you and loved the way you were growing. We both are just twenty-four at this time and preparing for a baby is a big task for us, but I am sure you will be a good girl or boy and will not trouble your mama.

I am not sure while writing this letter whether you are a girl or a boy, but I want you to be a girl, beautiful and intelligent like your mother.

When Ashima informed me about you, I had the same feeling in my stomach as I had when I saw your mother for the first time. She was an open book, but still a puzzle for me. Your growth in her womb is like the growth of my love towards my Angel.

Everyday my love for her increases, as you are developing inside. As you take nutrients from an umbilical cord, my love takes nutrients from her smile, laughter and hugs. That's why I call her Angel; she is the one because of whom I am living my life and you need to understand this today. Your mother has gone through a lot of changes and pain in the last few months, which you can not even imagine, but I know she did her best to bring you to this world.

Promise me something, my baby, that you will never hurt a girl; physically nor mentally. Because girls are real angels whom we can see in our life. You will never meet god, but believe me, if god exists, he does in girls.

You are the luckiest baby in this world who has got the best mama, and I am sure she will give you the best of the world, along with me. With this letter, I would like to share with you this rose. You'll ask why this dried rose? Come on now, do not make faces, because this is a symbol of feelings when you do something new for the first time. I gave this rose to your mother on our first Valentine's day after the proposal, and I can still feel the butterflies in my stomach. I could feel those butterflies again when I heard you are coming to our life and so this flower. Your mother kept it safely till now, which I have stolen today from her box to gift you. Do take care of this – it's not just a flower, it's a symbol of love and affection.

Today, I promise that we as your parents will make you smile forever, we as your parents will give you the best of your life, we as your parents will provide you with an experience to cherish.

Remember one last thing, 'There is only one happiness in life – to love and be loved.'

Your
Teddy Papa

With tears in her eyes, she finished reading the letter, kissed the rose and leaned back deep in thought. I kept observing her in pain as she spoke softly, "Baby you heard me? Your Papa wanted to do many things for you." She paused and then continued, "But now who will do all these things for us? Who will take care of us? Who will take me to a Chinese restaurant? Who will smile with us? Who will play with us?"

She asked many questions glowering to herself, placed the letter to her side and closed her eyes. That night she read the letter again and again, letting the pillow get wet with tears.

13

That letter became her oxygen for some days. She used to carry that letter along the whole day, as if she was feeling my presence. About a week later, the doorbell rang in the evening. Papa stood to open the door and found Sanjeev for a visit.

"Good evening uncle. Remember me, Dr Sanjeev?" He greeted Papa with folded hands.

"Oh yes, please come in."

Sanjeev stepped inside, followed by a girl and continued, "Uncle, she is my fiancee, Dr Rashmi."

Papa greeted her and asked both of them to sit. Papa's face was blank and he could not understand his reason to visit. While Sanjeev continued, "I was in school with Kartik and Ashima till twelfth, after which I shifted to Pune for my medical studies and lost contact. It was shocking to meet Kartik like this, but... I am sorry for your loss, Uncle."

"It's okay, beta. No one is above god's wish." Papa asked them to sit and continued, "Let me call his mother."

I also came outside and stood beside Sanjeev. Rashmi was a beautiful girl, and they both made a perfect couple. I still remember Sanjeev during our school days – he was a studious student, and we'd mostly find him in the library or in class buried in his books.

Time fills all gaps. Today Sanjeev was sitting at my place. His body language was suggesting that he wanted to help my family, but years back, I was the one who had slapped him. Today my soul was regretting that. People say correctly – you regret your deeds when you die. Now I know what karma is. Whatever wrong you do, you regret it after death as you can be in control of everything, but you cannot do anything to make amends.

I still remember our twelfth class days. I was with Ashima in the Arts section, whereas Sanjeev was in the Science section. He was the silent guy of his class, mostly being by himself. We never had any interaction with him till the time came to select the head boy and head girl of the school. The management thought Ashima and Sanjeev were best suited for the positions. I was very happy for Ashima; my love was the school head girl now.

But that position brought some changes in her. I understood responsibilities bring changes, and it was because of that. Ashima became busy in school and other activities. Most of the time she stayed back after school, and I had to drive back all alone. I started missing her. Before that, she was always with me from morning till I dropped her at her home in the afternoon. We studied together, ate together, cycled together. This sudden change began affecting me a lot.

And then one day, I overheard some of the students talking about the relationship between Sanjeev and Ashima, as most of the time in school and after school, they were together for some or the other activity. Doubt is the mother of all quarrels, and so this thought of Sanjeev taking away my love started poking me all the time. I could not concentrate on my studies for the fear of losing her.

But I was not wrong altogether. Sanjeev had started creating a unique space for Ashima in his heart, and that was quite obvious by his behaviour. I began observing him minutely, and jealousy began to fill my heart.

One evening, I got a call from Ashima. She wanted to meet urgently. Without wasting time, I cycled to her society. She was waiting at the gate and smiled as she saw me.

"What happened Ashima? Is everything fine?" I questioned leaving my cycle to fall to the ground.

She held my hand and pulled me to the side, "Listen Kartik, I have something to tell you, but promise me, you will not say this to anyone. I can only tell you as you are my best friend."

This best friend tag is the worst one if your best friend is of the opposite sex. My heartbeat was almost on the verge of stopping when she told me that Sanjeev had proposed to her. My first reaction was that I was such a fool. Being her best friend for the last two years, I still had not been able to propose to her. And here, a third person who had just known her for twenty days, had proposed to her.

"And what did you say?" I questioned with grave looks.

"I said I need time to think," she replied immediately. I looked to the other side and then questioned her back, "Do *you love her?" Actually, I didn't want to hear an answer to that question. What if she had said yes.*

"I don't know, Kartik," she replied. I relaxed because now I had time to manage things until she made up her mind. I gave her a friendly suggestion to concentrate on her studies as our board exams were nearing, but my mind was listing down options to stop this proposal.

And then after thinking for the whole night, I decided to talk to Sanjeev. Next day, during the lunch break, I reached out to him when Sanjeev was having his tiffin.

"Hey Sanjeev," I called him from behind.

"Hello Kartik, what's up man?"

"Tell me something?" I came straight to the point with a glowering look.

Looking at me, Sanjeev stood up and asked, "What happened, Kartik?"

I was taller and well built and this was sufficient to take a punch at him, if required.

"Did you propose to Ashima?" I questioned outright.

He was silent and tried to avoid me, but I questioned him again, "Did you propose to Ashima?" My eyes were fixed on him and then he replied, "Yes I did, because I love her a lot."

I don't know what happened next, but five guys and a few teachers had to pull me off from him, and his nose was a bloody mess, as I had smashed my fist right into his face. Within no time, I was standing in front of the Principal, and Sanjeev was sitting on the chair applying ice cubes to his nose.

"May I know what happened? Why did you hit him? It is against the rules of the school. You will be expelled for this!" the

Principal shouted. He could never tolerate indiscipline, and I had broken all the rules that day. I would be getting expelled.

He called his peon and asked him to type my expulsion letter. Sanjeev was crying in pain, and some of the teachers were helping him with medicines. I felt apologetic as I had hurt him a lot, but it was sudden rage that was uncontrollable.

Within no time, the peon came out with the printout of the expulsion letter. The principal took it and was about to sign it before calling my parents, when Sanjeev interrupted, "Sir, now I can speak. Please do not expel him."

"What? He hit you, and you are saving him?"

"Sir... he didn't hit me." Sanjvee replied thinking and continued still holding his nose, "Actually I was running in the corridor, and... and I slipped. My face hit the pillar at the corner, and thankfully, Kartik tried to hold me and stopped me from falling. At that moment, everyone entered and thought he had hit me."

I looked at him with a roguish look, as I knew he was telling a story to save me. But why, that was the question.

The principal also knew he was telling a lie, but he let me go with a warning, as Sanjeev stuck to his words. I never spoke to Sanjeev after that, and within a few months, he shifted to Pune with his parents.

On his last day, he came to me at the cycle stand of the school where I was standing alone and said, "We may never meet again in this life Kartik, but I would like to tell you something. I didn't tell a lie because I was afraid of you or because I do not love Ashima. I said a lie because I realized after proposing to her, that Ashima loves you more than anyone in this world, and I could *not be the reason to tear you both apart," he merely said and left, leaving me standing, my lips sealed.*

Today, after my death, he was sitting at my place. I wanted to hug him and say, 'I am sorry brother'. But it was too late now.

Sanjeev and Rashmi stood up as Mummy entered the room.

"Namaste Aunty. We thought we'd meet Ashima as she may need her friends at this tough time."

"Perfect beta, thanks for visiting. We are also worried about Ashima and her baby. Maybe she will feel better after interacting with her friends," Mummy replied.

"Will try my best, Auntyji. This is life, and we need to move on. Where is Ashima?" Sanjeev asked.

"She is in her room, let me check if she can join you," Mummy replied and walked to her room.

Ashima was busy looking at my old videos again and again on her mobile.

"Ashima beta, your friend Sanjeev is here to meet you. Would you like to meet him?" Mummy asked politely. Ashima didn't bother to reply and continued with her eyes on the video.

Mummy took a step forward and again asked, "Beta, are you coming?" This time, she looked up and nodded.

Mummy came back in some time and confirmed that she would be joining them shortly.

In the next few minutes, Ashima came out, her face ashen with swollen eyes, carrying a teddy bear in her hands. Her hair was a mess and her face expressionless. Sanjeev stood and hugged her gently, while she remained silent without giving any response. Rashmi also stood up, smiled at her and asked her to sit down. Ashima took a seat next to Sanjeev on the sofa, but seemed lost in her own world.

As Sanjeev gestured to Rashmi, she took a seat next to Ashima and told her, "Ashima, I am Dr Rashmi, and I am your friend Sanjeev's fiancée."

Ashima gave her a glazed look and started caressing her teddy bear. Rashmi understanding her situation started further, "I am a gynecologist. Can I give you a quick check-up? Let's see how your baby is doing." Hearing about the baby, Ashima nodded politely.

Rashmi, being a doctor, knew how to handle such cases of depression. Rashmi looked at my mummy, as she needed a room. Mummy showed her to Ashima's bedroom. Rashmi stood up holding Ashima and went to the room. As she went, Sanjeev said, "Uncleji, Rashmi is a very good gynecologist. I know Ashima is carrying a baby and the stress and pain in such a situation may affect her baby. I discussed this with Rashmi, and she said she would check her at home. We know you must be consulting some good doctor, but I asked Rashmi to start a conversation with Ashima by this means. It would help her to get friendly with her."

I was so thankful to Sanjeev for thinking about her. I stood and went into the room to see how our baby was doing.

"Ashima, can you show me your prescription?" Rashmi asked. Ashima pulled open the drawer and handed over the file of her pregnancy, without saying a word to her. "Please lie down on the bed and let me check you."

Rashmi pulled out her stethoscope from the bag and placed it on her stomach and chest. She then asked her to get up and started reading her file.

"Okay, good Ashima, you are doing great and so is your baby. You need to follow a few tips. You need to be happy and smiling. I could hear your baby saying 'Mama is so sad'. Get some fresh air and mingle with people. I am just adding Vitamin C and one more medicine to your prescription; everything else is fine. If you have any problem, give me a call. I am leaving my number on this prescription." Rashmi helped Ashima to stand and was about to leave when she saw my letters on the bed. "Oh, so you are reading something to keep yourself occupied?" Rashmi tried to pick one of the letters which were all folded and placed on the bed. But Ashima caught hold of her hand and gestured her to stop.

"Oh, I am sorry. Guess those are personal," Rashmi replied and then placed both her hands on Ashima's shoulders and told her, "You can consider me as your friend, your best friend, and I assure you, we together will bring back a smile on your face."

Ashima kept looking at her with a brooding expression.

"Okay, let's go to the living area." Rashmi held her hand and allowed her to walk slowly.

Sanjeev stood as he saw Rashmi coming out from the room.

"Okay Aunty, we will keep visiting," he said.

"Have some tea and biscuits, Betaji," Mummy offered.

"Thanks Auntyji, some other day. We both need to rush to the hospital," Sanjeev replied.

"Aunty, she is perfectly fine. I have added two more medicines. Please start those. And I have left my number in the prescription. Give me a call anytime," Rashmi told Mummy. Sanjeev then took a step closer to Ashima, and placing his left hand on her head he said, "Ashima, we will keep coming to see you, and if you need us, we are just a ring away."

Sanjeev and Rashmi took their leave and went downstairs. I don't know why but I followed them, as a gesture to drop them till their car.

"Sanjeev, she is having a disorder of the placenta. I have seen her report," Rashmi informed him as they were on the stairs.

"What? Is it in a critical stage or normal, which can get handled?"

"It was not so critical during the last ultrasound, and that's why her doctor suggested bed rest. But looking at her condition now, it could be a problem."

Hearing her talking about Ashima's health, I went along with them. Sanjeev started the vehicle and questioned, "Any particular observation?"

"Firstly, as per her dates, her seventh month has started, and it's the most critical month. It's the start of the third trimester, and there will be more discomfort than before. I am not sure how she will handle that as she is in depression," Rashmi replied.

"Her depression is worrying; I also observed that. She didn't speak a single word while we were there. She was one of the most talkative girls in school."

"That's why I added one antidepressant of mild strength, which won't affect her baby. But it was required," Rashmi confirmed.

"You did well. It will help, I think."

I got worried about my Angel, but was not sure what to do and how god would help us in this situation. Her placenta problem was my reason for worry when I was alive and now listening to Rashmi, my soul was also worried.

I returned home and saw Ashima standing in the balcony, and about to start reading the next letter of mine. She opened the letter with shaky hands.

My dearest Baby,

Congratulations on your second month! I am back with my next letter. You may not understand, but this is one of the best things I loved to do after you've entered our lives. You are now the size of a blueberry. You look like a curled up tube with one end of the tube becoming the head, and the other your bottom. Believe it or not, you have grown ten thousand times than what you were at conception. Your head is quite large, with a prominent forehead. Your ears, nose, eyes, and eyelids have begun to form. Soon tissues that form the heart will start to beat. By the end of the second month, you will grow to about two inches.

You will be wondering how I know all this? Am I also in your mother's womb? No, I read it in books which you will also enjoy when you grow up. It's my dream to make you rest on my shoulder every night and narrate a story from a fairy tale book. I assure you, Ashima and you will love it."

Ashima wiped her tears which were making her vision blurry and continued,

"Your second month is almost the same as my second year with your mother. Our friendship grew a thousand times more, and my heart started beating for her. My ears began to be active to hear her voice; my eyes began searching for her everywhere, my eyelids stopped blinking when she was near me, and I could sense her perfume from a distance.

With this letter, I have placed a red ribbon belonging to your mama. She used to wear it in school. Your mama looked stunning in two braids with red ribbons, and whenever I dreamet of her, she came to me with those ribbons in her hair. That day, I noticed that one of her ribbons was loose, as she walked in the corridor of the school. Something clicked my mind, and I decided I wanted to keep that ribbon with me forever. I walked towards her from the opposite side. I came closer, smiled, said hello and walked pulling her loose ribbon softly with my right hand, when her face was in the other direction. I folded the ribbon and placed it in my pocket. She did not know then and even today, that it was taken by me.

You'd be thinking what a thief my father is, but I would like to confess. I am not a thief; I am just too much in love with her. I want to keep everything which will serve as a memory to me of the most memorable time I have spent with your mother. She is my heartbeat which I would like to hide within. Her every small thing is a memory for me. I want to save every breath she takes, and want to keep every smile she smiles.

I hope I won't be jealous of you because you would be sharing her with me, but I know I will love it because you are the real love which I have given her.

Promise me something on the first day of the second month, that you will love your mama more than I do; promise you will make her smile even when I am not near; promise me you will respect us.

You would be thinking I am such a harsh father, who is taking so many promises even when you are just a couple of months old, but these are the promises which I am assuming from you, but I know it's me who needs to fulfill them along with you. We both will be working as a team, to make our love the happiest person in this world.

Champ, this is all for this month. Come fast, I am waiting for a party with you!

Yours,
Teddy Papa

Ashima closed the letter and started thinking with tears in her eyes. I remained standing next to her and could understand her feelings. She was missing me so much. She started caressing her stomach. I could see a tear drop slowly rolling down from her left eye, reaching to her ears and disappearing into her thick black hair. Years back, I had promised myself that I would never let her eyes get wet. And that day, I was the only reason for the flood in her heart.

She went inside our room taking long steps and started searching for something in the cupboard. When I reached closer to her, she stopped, and started looking at me as if she felt me standing close. A wave moved in my soul realizing she felt my presence. She paused for a second and then again started searching for something. I could still see the tears in her eyes; they started rolling down much faster. Her hands began moving quickly, scattering the clothes all over the room. She turned, and her hand smashed the pen holder placed in the corner of the desk. Something was going on in her mind, which I was not able to guess. She then pulled out her wedding sari which was red with golden work. I was still wondering what she was up to, but then my worst nightmare was in front of me. She took the support of the bed corner and tried to stand on the bed. Oh what, what was she doing? Was she trying to commit suicide? Yes, she was working on it. Oh god please help. Give me some powers for a few minutes, let me save her. Let me save my Angel and our baby. Someone must stop Ashima; she could not do this!

She threw the sari towards the fan and started tying a knot. She pulled the sari and checked if it was tightly hanging on the fan. I started shouting, *"Ashima, Angel, stop! Do not do this. It's excruciating. Think about our baby; stop dear, please!"*

I was crying in pain, but no way I could stop her. She continued making a loop of the sari against her neck and then placed three pillows one above the other. I rushed outside towards the room of my parents and started shouting at them to help her. I was screaming, but no one was listening. I wanted to touch my parents and let them know what she was up to, but being a soul was pathetic. I was rushing from one room to another, finding ways to save her. Within minutes, I don't know how, I was at Sanjeev's place. I started calling him for help, I tried to bang on his table, I decided to move things, but nothing worked. I came back to my home. But could not gather the strength to watch her die, along with our baby. I moved back to my parent's room; they were busy talking. I continued yelling, tried my best to reach them, but with no response. I went to the corner crying without tears and sat hiding my face with my hands.

I placed my hand on my chest; I could feel the frigid cold surrounding my heart, so I knew it was there, but lately, I couldn't feel it beating anymore. Some say you find purpose in the simplicity of your heartbeat; I realized ghosts have no intent to roam around as they do not have a heart. When we are alive, we say our feelings are in the heart, but how come the soul feels it when the heart gets burnt to ashes? I was afraid, I guessed. I was worried about my Angle; was fearful for our baby who had still not seen the light of the world. I was not breathing anymore, but stillness filled the icy air in my heart. I wish I could punch a hole in a wall and turn a table over; hope I could hold her back and save my love. But I couldn't. I merely sat there, letting the numbness and anger take me.

I kept sitting there sobbing and waiting for the soul of my Angel to enter with my baby in her arms. I could see the day getting over and darkness taking over the light. After sometime, Papa and Mummy stood up and started their regular work, without checking what Ashima was up to in her room. I was afraid of finding her dead and could not gather the strength to check myself.

After a while, Mummy went to her room with a cup of tea. I followed her with fear. Papa switched on the lights of the living area saying that it was really dark, and they had forgotten to turn on the lights before. I continued to follow Mummy and waited as she knocked Ashima's room door. Mummy paused for a few seconds and then pushed the door.

I could see Mummy's feet stop; her face turned pale. I came out from behind to look at the body of my love, but to my relief, Angel was alive. But she was sitting wearing that red sari. She was dressed as a bride, with swollen eyes, badly put make-up and her hair in one braid tied up with a red ribbon. Mummy could not understand what to say or how to react, except letting her tears flow. She wiped her tears with the border of her sari, controlling her tears. She put on a plastic smile and said, "Wow! Ashima, you are looking so nice. Lovely beta." Mummy placed the cup of tea and picked up the kajal from the dressing table saying,

"Let me apply some Kajal to you, it will keep you safe from evil eye."

Ashima turned her neck to the side and took her blessings. But I knew what was going on in her mind. The way she had got dressed was proof of the depression she was undergoing. Mummy smiled and went outside, leaving her alone and cried hiding her tears. I went up to Ashima and went down on my knees looking into her eyes to say, "Angel, I am the most unlucky person who can see the most beautiful creation of god, but cannot raise my hands to touch it. I am sorry for the state you are in, but it's me who is in pain finding your tears flowing for me. Forgive me, my Angel."

I spoke to her and stood up to go outside to hear what Mummy was conveying to Papa. "We need to take her to the doctor. If this continues, it will affect her baby," Mummy explained to Papa sobbing.

"I think it's better to discuss this with Sanjeev. He will help us," Papa suggested picking up his mobile.

14

The next day, Sanjeev and Rashmi visited our house in the evening. Sanjeev requested Papa if he could take Ashima along with them for dinner. It would be good if she spent some time with friends. This would help to bring some change in her attitude. Papa allowed it without a second thought. Rashmi entered her room after knocking and tried to be friendly.

"Ashima, what are you doing? C'mon, get ready fast. I am starving," Rashmi said, taking a seat next to her on the bed.

Ashima kept looking at her with innocent eyes before replying softly, "Let me ask mummyji to serve you daal and rice. She cooks delicious food." Though in a low sad voice, Rashmi was happy as Ashima had responded.

"No, we are not eating at home. Will be having dinner outside," Rashmi replied convincingly.

"No. I am not sure if Kartik has eaten his food or not. How can I enjoy?" Ashima replied with concern.

Hearing her, Rashmi took a seat next to her and placed her hands on her shoulders and replied, "Ashima, you need to understand that this is life, and we must move on. If not for yourself, move on for your baby."

Ashima looked at her innocently, while Rashmi continued, "And don't worry, I will check if Kartik has had his dinner. Now get ready, darling!"

Ashima paused and then stood up, but stopped, turned and asked again, "Are you sure? Kartik will have his dinner?"

"Sure darling. I will ask Sanjeev to check. You get ready, I am waiting for you in the living area," Rashmi tried to be normal and stepped outside.

"Is she coming?" Sanjeev questioned as Rashmi stepped out from the room. She nodded and took a seat next to Sanjeev.

"Auntyji, Ashima is in profound shock. We need to bring her out of this. In such a situation, she may harm the baby also, as she is careless. You need to take care of her," Rashmi explained to Mummy.

I stood behind my mother and listened to what Rashmi was explaining. I was worried for Ashima and so was everyone sitting in that room. After a few minutes, the door opened and Ashima walked outside, wearing a long gown with flowers printed on it. She looked disheveled even though she had tried putting on some make-up. She was nowhere close to her normal self, yet I was just happy to see her come out of her room after ages.

Without saying a word to anyone, she opened the main door and started climbing down the stairs while everyone looked at her in silence. Sanjeev and Rashmi quickly joined her after saying bye to my parents.

"Take care of her, beta," Mummy replied from behind.

Reaching her, Sanjeev unlocked the car and opened the front seat door for Ashima. Ashima stopped and then got into the back seat saying, "I only sit in the front seat with Kartik."

Sanjeev gave a thoughtful look and asked Rashmi to sit with her behind.

"So, we are going to a pub called Imperfecto that has just newly opened in Noida. Have you been there before, Ashima?" Sanjeev questioned while driving. Ashima kept looking out of the window as if she was seeing the scenery for the first time in her life. She remained silent as if she had not heard him. Rashmi placed her hand on her shoulders and questioned her again on behalf of Sanjeev. Ashima just nodded absentmindedly.

In no time, we reached Imperfecto pub. With dim lights, the sound of the live band was loud enough to drown the soul. Couples were sitting in every corner, laughing and enjoying their drinks. The music was as loud as thunder; it made the cutlery on the tabletops rattle. Neon lights flashed everywhere like police sirens, but were much more colourful. There was no dance floor, but everyone was dancing to the rhythm. Sanjeev asked Rashmi and Ashima to go inside and take a seat, while he walked to the counter to have a word with the manager, who was his friend. I remained standing in the crowd, trying to understand the silence within my soul which could not be penetrated by the loud music of the live band.

I remained standing as I got lost in the crowd, trying to search for answers for the numerous questions in my mind.

Who was I now? Why was I still roaming the earth? If I loved Ashima, why was I worried about her committing suicide? Soon every page of my life started turning in front of my eyes in the darkness. Looking at every smiling face, I could remember happy times with my Angel; with every laugh, I started remembering the best times we had spent together; with every kiss, I started remembering the passionate kisses we shared.

And then I came out from my illusion when I saw Rashmi rushing towards Sanjeev saying something. Sanjeev looked tense and rushed outside. I pushed past the crowd and ran behind him. I soon realized that Aashima was not in the pub. She had left when Rashmi had gone to the washroom. Sanjeev ran downstairs while Rashmi again ran inside to check. I also started searching for her, letting my eye move to every corner of the pub. Rashmi rushed outside, following Sanjeev.

"Did you check the washroom?" Sanjeev questioned.

"Ya, I did. Did you call her?" Rashmi shouted from behind to Sanjeev.

"Yes, trying but she is not picking up my call," Sanjeev replied with the mobile placed on his ear. I also started rushing behind them. Sanjeev took the lift and reached the ground floor.

"Let's go in different directions and find her; she would not have gone far," Rashmi suggested.

They both started running in different directions. Rashmi was trying to find her in the open air restaurants, while Sanjeev ran to the exit gate, to talk to the security guards. Sanjeev scanned the crowd in the mall and realized he could not see her. He started to walk amongst the families, his eyes darting more wildly with each passing second, noticing if any pregnant girl in a long evening gown was around. Then he began to call her name loudly, until many heads turned in his direction. He had their attention. He might as well use it. "Has anyone seen a pregnant girl in a long gown?" he yelled, his voice almost cracking.

The sea of blank faces stared back at him. Sanjeev was trying his best to find her and so was Rashmi. Rashmi was trying to find her in every corner of the mall, in the women's wear and kid's section, but in vain.

I was feeling helpless, as I could not do anything other than run behind them. I always believed life was complicated, but then realized I was in a more puzzled phase for my soul. I placed my hands on my head and began to think and pray to god to take care of my family. My eyes were still moving in every direction, and then I felt helpless for not being to locate her. Weak, I looked up at the sky and found it was a night without the moon. Twinkling stars tried to compete with the light of the busy metro city. Looking at the stars, I recalled something and remembered that Ashima loved watching stars. It was entirely possible she would be sitting in a quiet place admiring them. I started going in the directions where she could probably be and then reached the open garden at the back of the mall. There was a lush green carpet of grass, and the light on the top of the pole mast at the center illuminated the colourful flowers. And amidst it sat my Angel with her head up, watching the stars.

I rushed towards her and took a seat next to her. I looked at her and found her beautiful eyes unblinking observing the stars. After sometime, she picked up her purse and opened it to pull out the next letter of mine.

Slowly, she opened the letter and laid it on the grass, while I lay next to her, again as her husband, admiring my most beautiful wife. I placed my shoulder below her head, to give her the comfort which none of us could feel, but still, I felt the closeness of her breath. She opened the letter and started reading it in the silence of her breath.

My dearest Baby,

Hope by now you can recognize me better. Yes, I am your father. Congratulations for completing the third month of your existence. This month you will be coming closer to us as we'll be hearing your heartbeat and will get a chance to have your first look during the ultrasound.

I am really very excited about that. I will raise my hand and say Hi! You must reply. I will be giving you a flying kiss in expectation of one back.

You are a grown-up baby now – the size of a lemon. Okay sorry, I am not laughing at you. I am so excited at the thought of seeing you come out from your mother's belly. Everyday I dream to carry you in my arms and kiss you on your nose. I want you to hold my fingers and make me feel how grown up I am.

Okay, one more important thing I want to tell you. Daily, I kiss your mama in the morning, during the evening and many times when I am near her. So make it clear, you need not have any confusion later, because that I will continue and will never stop. But I ensure you will get equal number of kisses as your mama.

You'll be wondering where is the hidden gift in this letter. So for this letter the hidden gift is the air. The air which touched me after touching your mama. The wind, which we felt while watching the stars at night; the air which we feel in our breath; the air which lets your mama's beautiful hair go crazy.

Whenever your mama is close to me, I feel a fragrance in the air, and today I captured it in this letter for you. You must always remember in your life, that you should create positive vibes in the air around you, which will make you smile and everyone else smile too.

You must become a person like your mama, who lets the direction of air turn towards her. Her presence can make flowers bloom and make the atmosphere vibrant.

My life is filled with love and joy having her close to me; I want you to feel the same and respect the same when you hug her with love.

This letter is short, but not the story of our love. Will tell you everything about our relationship once you are with us.

And one more promise I want to make to you today. I will try to be the best Dad for you; will let you do what you want to do; will let you live your life; will find happiness in your smiles. But you need to promise me one thing. You need to make my love, my Angel, smile forever in her life.

Love you a lot,
Teddy Papa

Holding the letter, she continued observing the night sky, unblinking. Her silence was speaking more than words.

The coming moment is the dream, while the moment gone is yours; we live in that past, searching for the lights of our memories. I remained sitting by her side in the silence of love when I saw Sanjeev running towards her. With heavy breaths he stood by her, placing his hands on his waist.

Seeing him, Angel stood up slowly, placed the letter back in the purse, and without speaking a word, walked past him. Sanjeev kept on looking at her, turned and then followed her. He understood her behaviour being a doctor. Sanjeev pulled his mobile and called Rashmi to come to the parking area.

Ashima has always been a giver – warm and loving. When she was a child, she never cried, seeking to make me happy. Often people sought her in times of trouble, and she gave everyone all she had – her whole heart and showered all her love upon them. She had never felt more empty in mind, body, and soul. Never so bereft of any comfort. Ashima had never felt so worthless or disposable, never so wretched and cold. For hours she would have no emotions, only an urge to keep watching the stars. Days became weeks and months, and in every single moment of every single day, her soul asked god why she was still alive. And, she would reply, "Because I love you, my baby, and you are my love."

They had their dinner in a different restaurant that evening, a place more silent and less crowded before Sanjeev dropped Ashima back home.

15

After a few days, Papa visited Rashmi's clinic to get an update about Ashima's health as her eighth month was about to start, and he could not see any improvement in her health and behaviour. Every day, she was delving into further depression. She wasn't eating well, and had almost stopped speaking to anyone. I was worried, but had no option than to watch her in pain and being in pain myself.

"Beta, I am terribly worried for Ashima. I thought I'd discuss this with you and show you her latest ultrasound report," Papa told Rashmi, as she was reading her reports.

Rashmi placed the report back, noted some critical points in her prescription and then replied, "Uncle, I can understand your concern. Being her friend, I want her to recover soon, but as you see, things are not improving. Her placenta problem is still there, and we need to be extra cautious during her delivery.

I could have recommended her to a consultant for therapy, but I have seen her closely. She will not agree to let go of the memories of Kartik, and if we try hard and force her, she may do something terrible."

Papa kept looking into her eyes, pleading and helpless. Rashmi placed her hand on Papa's hand and replied, "Uncle, we together can bring a difference; we as a family need to bring her out from this trauma. Once her delivery gets completed, we can start some therapies for her. But at this moment, we just need to keep her relaxed."

Papa stood holding the back of the chair without saying anything and turned to walk, when Rashmi again said from behind, "Uncle, I am sure we will bring her back to her old self soon."

I could see that Papa's eyes were wet, but he held back his tears, joined his hands in namaste helplessly. Papa was not so aged, but my death had made him lifeless, and age had taken over his appearance. It was not only Ashima who was depressed, but the people who needed to help her were also depressed.

It was evening when Papa reached home. He sat in the nearby park. He moved slowly to the bench where I once used to place cards. The sound of feet dragging on the grass could be heard as he walked lost in thoughts. The atmosphere was windy, and the fragrance of the vegetation filled the air. Few children were busy playing cricket at the center of the park, while many joggers were on their run. Papa touched the backrest of the bench with trembling hands and took a seat. Papa removed his big cream spectacles and started wiping them with the help of his shirt, as I took a seat next to him. I could see his swollen wet eyes, lost in my memories. He was my role model, my hero, but that day I could see him failing. Not only because I had died, but because he not could get the old Ashima back.

While he was busy thinking, a cricket ball came towards him and passed by his side towards the back of the bench, into the bushes.

"Uncleji, can you throw our ball?" A young boy from a distance asked.

"Wait, let me throw it," Papa replied with a pause and stood from his seat. He was crazy about cricket, and I knew he would love to feel the ball in his hands after a very long time. We used to play cricket when I was six or seven years old. He moved with controlled steps and leaned to look for the ball in the bushes, but after a few seconds, he stopped. His hands stopped moving, his body got still, and then a warm drop of tear rolled down his cheek as he found one of the crushed letters of mine behind the bushes. He picked up the rolled piece of paper, forgetting about the ball. Soon a small boy came running and moved to pick his ball, while Papa kept looking at the paper ball. He strolled back to the bench, trying to open the paper ball. At that moment he could only hear the sound of the crumpled paper as he unfolded it. A month of lying behind the bushes had made it rough, dirty and the colour had faded. Still, it was one of the best gifts Papa had received that day, which was visible in his eyes. Wish he would have had read that on the day when I had sent it to him; hope he would have hugged me on the day when I wanted to be close to him. I would be sitting alive then.

He unwrapped the paper roll and tried to read with his old eyes, but he could not understand a word of those faded letters. He caressed that paper as if he was loving me and then folded it to place it back in his pocket. After waiting for some more minutes in silence among the sounds of nature, he turned to leave for home.

It was seven in the evening and darkness had taken over. With his shivering old hands, he switched on the lights of the corridor. As Papa walked, his floaters made a sound of friction which was the only sound that could be heard in that silence. He opened the door and entered the silent house, which was once called home. Mummy was in the kitchen busy with preparation for the evening dinner. The sound of the utensils was sufficient to let others know the house was not empty. I moved into my bedroom to check on Ashima. She was sitting alone. Her hair had not been combed for days, her tears had stopped but not the pain, and she was lost in herself with one hand on her belly. I was worried about looking at her, as the problem with the placenta was still there and she was not taking care of herself at all.

I placed myself next to her as she opened the next letter from the box. She rubbed her eyes to wipe away the tears, and kissed it before beginning as if trying to feel my presence. And then she began to read:

Hello, my Baby,

How are you doing dear? First of all, a big hug and love to you. Everyday when you are moving in your mother's belly, I get really excited to write the next letter to you. And let me tell you, a smile on your mother's face is the most beautiful ornament she wears. Since we were in school, I kept looking at her unblinking, to capture every moment of her smile. I bet, you will never find such a beautiful smile in the whole world.

I wish I could make her smile forever and ever. And junior, it's your responsibility to make her happy and to smile along with me. The day I saw her, I loved her; the day I loved her, I decided to make her smile forever.

Today, I am gifting you this smiley sticker which you must place on our dressing table mirror so that you remember... that you need to make her smile. And I promise, if your mama smiles, I will smile, and our family will smile. So from now onwards, it's not only my responsibility, but it will be team work, to spread the smiles in our home. Our home of love.

Catch you later, junior. Keep smiling and make my Angel smile!

Bye.

Love you,
Your Teddy Pap

Ashima finished the letter and closed her eyes. She remained silent, feeling our baby within. Then she opened her eyes and inhaling a lot of oxygen, she moved her hand to the box and pulled out the yellow coloured smiley sticker. A sticker of something which she had forgotten in her life. Holding her stomach, she tried to lift herself from the bed; placing her feet in her slippers at the end of the bed and strolled towards the mirror. I kept watching her, as she stood in front of the mirror.

She then moved her hands in front of her face and stuck the sticker on the mirror. She kept looking at it for a few seconds before she smiled, caressing her stomach.

Ashima was smiling. Yes, she was smiling.

Perhaps a smile wasn't the right word for it. The top row of teeth was showing, and there was a faint curve to the lips, but there was no smile in her eyes, and no movement of the cheeks. She was smiling a little, a smile with a twist to it, like the smile of a child who is determined to not weep. But even that smile was a ray of hope for me.

I had seen her smiling for the first time since my death, and that was the day, my soul felt relaxed. I thought I had drunk a glass of chilled water after a long time of thirst. Ashima then turned and walked outside, opening the door to let the dining room light enter her room. She saw Mummy serving Papa dinner on the dining table.

Mummy turned in astonishment, as after a long time, Ashima had opened the door by herself. Before Mummy could say a word, Ashima smiled at her, saying, "Mummy, let me help you with dinner."

Mummy looked at Papa with a smile and moved to hold Ashima saying, "Dinner is ready beta, you come here and have a seat. Would you like to have dinner with us today?" Mummy asked. Ashima nodded and took a seat pulling out a dining table chair. Mummy was about to go to the kitchen to bring something, when Ashima interrupted, "Mummy, please sit with me and have your dinner. It would be nice."

Mummy placed her hand on Ashima's head and took a seat. Papa meanwhile was avoiding eye contact with her. Ashima turned the plate positioned in front of her as Mummy served her some rice and rajma. Everyone was still silent when Ashima picked the remote of the television and switched it on and flipped channels to stop at Tom & Jerry. Papa turned his face slightly to check what she was watching on television and continued to eat his food.

"You like cartoons, beta?" Mummy questioned Ashima.

"Well, till Kartik was there, he made me smile and laugh. I think I'll need these probes now," Ashima replied with her eyes stuck on the television screen. Mummy had no words to reply to her and then Ashima continued, "Mummy, you know Kartik always said, a smile is a multivitamin dose which everyone must have the whole day."

"Yes beta, and that is so true," Mummy replied.

Ashima placed her hand on Mummy's hand and looking into her eyes replied, "I am trying to smile, Mummy, to feel him smiling. He said once, 'I smile because you are smiling and will die the day you stop smiling'." Ashima paused, kept looking into her eyes and then continued, "He died mummy, although I always smiled till he was with me." And her eyes filled up with tears ready to flow out. She moved her hands and rubbed her eyes, tilting her neck back to stop them from flooding.

Mummy stood and hugged her, "Ashima, we will smile and make him smile if he could see us from heaven."

Papa kept listening to everything which was going on but was silent in his guilt.

That night, Ashima continued watching television the whole night. I remained seated beside her as she continued to laugh, smile and cry watching cartoons. That day I realized why children watch cartoons – it's not because they loved the story, but they liked to laugh on their own. That day she smiled again and so did I. Her voice could be heard in other rooms making Papa and Mummy relax a bit. I was smiling because finally my love was smiling. I stood and moved to the bedroom and stood in front of the mirror in which I could not see my reflection, but could see the sticker stuck on it.

16

Ashima was still sleeping after a whole night of smiles and laughter. I lay beside her, observing her the entire night. Her cheeks might be hurting from smiling for so long, but I could not kiss them and relax. The corner of her lips fought to fall to reveal her true feelings as she slept. But I knew that if she had decided, she would not let that happen, after realizing that this is what I wanted. I was not sure if she would be able to carry a smile in reality and play the 'happy girl' image for long. But I believed if she could only continue it for a few more days, she might get out of the pain she was in, and our baby would be born healthy.

It was noon when her phone rang. Ashima was in deep sleep and not bothered about picking up the phone. It kept on ringing for a while. After a few more rings, Ashima moved her hand to the alarm clock and tried to switch it off, without knowing it was her phone which was ringing. Later, she picked it up, her eyes still closed, "Hello?"

"Oh my darling Ashima, get up baby. I heard you smiled?" Rashmi exploded from the other end with excitement.

"Hi Rashmi, thanks for calling… hun.. yes, I tried," Ashima replied in her drowsiness. But at least she was speaking.

"What do you mean by trying? It's something you must start practicing every moment now."

"By the way, how did you come to know about it?" Ashima questioned her in a low voice.

"Hun… no guesses. I called Auntyji a few minutes back, and she informed me. She was really happy for you," Rashmi informed her.

Ashima was silent for a second. She opened her eyes, pulled herself up a little to be comfortable and replied, "Kartik wanted me to smile, so am trying to be his best obedient wife."

"Lovely! Now get ready. We're going out. I will be reaching in half an hour," Rashmi replied.

"No, I am comfortable at home." Ashima showed her unwillingness to go out. "And you know my problem of the low lying placenta," Ashima concluded.

But Rashmi was not in a mood to listen to anything, "Madam, I am a qualified gynaecologist, and I am with you as your live hospital, so do not worry. I am reaching, be ready."

"But where are we going?" Ashima questioned again but Rashmi disconnected the call saying, "Just be ready."

Ashima smiled as she stood up from the bed carefully, and this time it was not fake. She yawned and placed her hand on her stomach to say, "Good morning, Baby."

She then went in front of the mirror rubbing her eyes and then placed her hand on the smiley sticker saying to me, "Teddy, I will smile, for you to remember I still love you."

I replied, "My Angel, I love you too."

Ashima moved to the washroom, and after a few minutes, the doorbell rang. It was Rashmi at the door.

"Welcome Betaji, how are you?" Mummy asked opening the door.

"I am perfectly fine, Auntyji. Where is the smiling diva?" Rashmi asked laughing. Rashmi had a very different attitude towards life. She was jolly by nature and loved everyone around. She hardly knew Ashima, but her care for her was genuine. She would not let her *doctor wala attitude* come in between her attention.

"I think she is in the washroom; you wait for sometime I will check," Mummy replied.

"Wait, Aunty." Rashmi stopped and took her into the living room. Quietly she explained, "Auntyji, I had observed a good sign of improvement when I talked to her today. This is what we needed. Her delivery is near, and she needs physical and mental strength both to deliver a baby. We need to be her strength now."

Mummy without saying any word, placed her hand on her face in love and smiled.

"Hello, Rashmi." Ashima's soft husky voice could be heard. She came out, dressed in a white floral gown, with no makeup and uncombed hair. But she was smiling, to show everyone that she was smiling for me.

Rashmi walked towards her and hugged her saying, "My lovely girl, you look beautiful dear."

"Thanks, where are we going?" Ashima questioned.

"Do not worry; I am not going to kidnap you, baby," Rashmi replied placing her hand on Ashima's shoulder.

"And your hospital today?" Ashima questioned.

"My OPD is in the evening, and I am still not married to take care of my husband. So it's free time," Rashmi replied laughing.

As they both walked towards the stairs, Mummy stared smiling. "Take care, beta."

The weather was perfect that day, with slight showers. The wind was calm. It was an ideal day to hang out. Rashmi drove her silver sedan towards the Garden Galleria Mall, and soon they both reached the restaurant, The Time Machine.

The restaurant was designed with the theme of time travellers and watches. Perfect ambience and decoration, lively and energetic. Rashmi chose that restaurant to bring life to the dead soul of Ashima.

They took a seat at the side of the lobby, from where the outside view was marvelous. Ashima was silently observing the outside world, as if she was seeing it for the first time. Rashmi kept looking at her while she drank a glass of water, and then interrupted the silent Ashima lost in thoughts.

"I am happy that you are trying to get normal."

Ashima turned to listen to her and then smiled. Playing with a water droplet on the glass, she replied. "I am trying to do what Kartik would have wanted me to do."

"Good, I loved that you recall what Kartik wanted you to do, and you are taking it in a positive way. So what more did he expect from you?" Rashmi asked placing her mobile back in her purse.

"I don't know?" Pause. "What more did he desire from me," Ashima answered again looking at the sparrow sitting outside on the ledge of the mall.

Ashima took a long pause and then continued, "Kartik wrote some letters to our baby."

Rashmi looked at her with curious eyes.

"He started writing letters to our baby which he wanted to give me as a surprise when I would walk in with our baby. He wanted our baby to know how his father felt during these nine months and how much he loved me." With a pause and a sip of water, she concluded, "I am just decoding his words of happiness for our baby."

Rashmi placed her hand on Ashima's palm and replied softly, "You are doing what he wanted perfectly. It's destiny. Destiny made him write those letters which are helping you today."

Ashima's eyes were getting wet as she started thinking about me again. But with a smile on her face, she tried to hide her pain and tears.

Rashmi ordered some delicious Indian food, and they continued with the conversation.

"How is Sanjeev? And when are you both planning to get married?" Ashima questioned after taking a bite.

"Ah. He is fine. Today he had morning OPD." With a pause as she took a bite continued, "And do not ask me about our marriage. Doctors can never marry on time," Rashmi replied frustrated.

"What does that mean?"

"We both have decided to complete our MS first and then will tie the knot, but yes, let me tell you one more secret." Rashmi smiled and came closer to murmur.

"We are planning to live in. We care for each other; we love each other and we have sex, so only the official stamp is left. So we've decided to move in together." Rashmi then stopped as she felt awkward showing excitement, maybe.

"A good decision," Ashima confirmed, not letting her feel the awkwardness.

"I am sorry if I showed over excitement and let you remember Kartik," Rashmi confessed.

"No. Not at all." With a pause. "I am happy to listen, as I felt nostalgic remembering our days when we were going to be married."

"Hello ma'am, may I serve you anything else?" the waiter interrupted in between.

"No. nothing, thanks," Rashmi confirmed. Ashima was playing with a spoon, rolling the rice on her plate before she continued to narrate, "Kartik's parents were not happy with our marriage. Let me be more precise – Kartik's father never liked me, and considered me as the reason for the differences between his son and him. Kartik came back from Dehradun informing them that he will marry me, but he was not sure how. And I knew him; he would have cried in pain if his parents would not have been present at our wedding."

"So did they come?" Rashmi questioned.

"My parents went to Dehradun and tried to convince them. I was not so happy about that, as Kartik's papa said some unwanted words to my father. But I remained silent for my Teddy.

"We both may not be right, but what to do when you are in love, you never see wrong."

Rashmi looked into her eyes, "I don't think you both were wrong. You both made a perfect couple."

Ashima looked outside and with a pause replied, "Yes, we were the perfect couple."

Rashmi further questioned, "So did his parents attend your wedding?"

"Ya, we had a big fat wedding, but Papa was just a spectator in it."

"And what about Kartik? He didn't try convincing him?" Rashmi further questioned.

"He tried once, but then let him be on his own, finding that he was adamant," Ashima explained, paused and concluded, "Kartik was unhappy with his father's attitude, but the happiness of our relation overtook that unhappiness."

That day, amidst the talks of love and life, over a table of good food, Ashima learned to smile and make new friends. But her life was going to be challenging and she needed to be prepared for all.

17

I always remembered the day of my marriage, which was planned in Chakrata as both families have their relatives there. Mummy was very active at my wedding, but Papa was missing from all the enjoyment. He went to Mussourie saying he had some urgent work.

My best friend, my father, was angry with me, and this was something which was bothering me a lot.

Ashima and her family were staying in the same Railway Colony in one of her father's friend's home. Everyone was excited and lost in the fun and enjoyment of the marriage rituals. The night before our marriage, I decided to meet Ashima the same way as I used to chase her during our school days.

It was one in the morning when I slipped out from my bedroom, hiding from all the relatives who were sleeping in almost every corner of the house. I moved with nimble feet among the line of mattresses spread all over the living room. I took out my cycle, which was full of dust, and drove to the Railway Colony. Hiding behind the main gate, I called Ashima on her mobile.

Just after a single ring, she picked it up, as if she had been waiting for my call.

"Were you waiting for my call?" I questioned.

"Teddy, I have been with you since the last seven years. I can read your mind. Wait, I am coming down," Ashima replied with a smile on her face.

"And you know this as well that I am outside your society gate?"

"You cannot hide anything from your wife," she tried to be naughty. I put the phone back, and I kept waiting for her in the cold night of November. Chakrata is closer to the hills and nights are always chilly.

Then after a few minutes, I could hear the sound of an anklet, soft and sweet. I turned to check and found that the moon had come down to earth. My Angel was dressed in a red and yellow lehenga, with her hair open. She was wearing anklets and bangles looking like the perfect bride.

I could not take my eyes off her, as she walked in the moonlight towards me with her eyes down. She was adjusting her earrings with her hand as she came by my side. Without speaking a word, she presented her ear to my face, to let me understand that her earrings needed to be tightened. We both knew each other so well that many times we didn't need to speak – our gestures were sufficient. I ran my fingers through her long curly hair and found her earrings. Her perfume was mesmerizing, and I found myself getting lost in her beauty. I have seen her almost everyday for the last seven years, but that day she looked most beautiful, as she was soon going to be Mrs Kartik.

"Will you stop staring at me, Teddy?"

"Wish I could, but eyes are not ready to blink," I confessed. Angel smiled and pushed me politely.

"Let's cycle till school," she said.

She took a seat in the front of my cycle.

"Keep your lehenga safe from the cycle pedals," I said as we rode on.

She tried to pull her lehenga a little and then turned her face to adjust her long curly hair to the side of her shoulder. We were riding along the curved road of Chakrata, with tall trees lining the road, fireflies glittering in the moonlight and the merry sound of the beetles. As we rode ahead, the full moon emerged in front of us, as if our road was going to land us right on it.

And then my eyes went to her, precisely her back. Ashima was wearing a backless top and her back looked fair and smooth in the moonlight. I could not resist myself from staring at her back; she looked so beautiful. I was proud that I was going to be her husband.

My cycle was going down the slope fast even when I was not pedaling. The cycle took a swift turn, and so my face touched her back, and I kissed her softly. She stiffened but pretended as if she had not noticed my kiss. I kept on pedalling, taking another turn and planting the next kiss on her back, this time more soft and polite. I could hear her moan in that silence of the night and then I tried to touch her. She leaned herself on my chest, allowing me to kiss her. I got lost in her beauty, tilting my face towards her soft glossy lips to kiss her. We were moving fast with our lips entangled, lost in each other and then, the cycle slipped, rolling us to the side, and we fell to the side in the grass.

She was below me in my arms unhurt and still lost in me, and so was I. I kept looking at her unblinking. We could hear our breathing which was fast and passionate by then, and I kissed her again, moving my lips into hers with my chest buried in hers. I caressed her face with my left hand, while she continued feeling me with her hands on my back. Initially, the kiss was slow and smooth, to feel each other's presence, and believe, that yes, we were one. Then it moved fast, eating each other's lips to let our souls meet along with our bodies. That road used to be empty in the daytime, so during the night, we were carefree. I moved my face to kiss her neck, making her moan. She ran her fingers through my hair, pushing my face into hers. I could smell her fragrance and wanted to get lost in it. And then a soft husky voice said, "I love you, Teddy."

Our kisses got faster and more passionate as we wanted each other desperately. My hands were moving fast to feel her entire body and then she slapped my hand as I was about to move to her thighs.

"Stop, Mr Husband, our wedding night is tomorrow!" She pushed me to her side. I was still breathing hoarsely lying by her side on the grass. We then turned our faces towards each other and then kissed again. We did not want to leave each other, not for a second, but we knew our boundaries and stopped to control ourselves just for a day longer.

"Why you are wearing this lehenga at night?" I questioned lying to her side.

"To ask you if it is looking fine on me," she replied.

"And you were sure that I would come tonight?" I questioned.

"Yes, because your cousins called me as soon as you left and teased me that you were out to meet me." She laughed.

"Holly shit. So they all know I am with you?" I replied in shock.

"Yes," she replied with a smile and hugged me. That night, we remained with each other for almost two hours, side by side, truly, madly, deeply in love.

She was a magnet. I could not resist going closer to her, and so my soul was still with her after my death. Still trying to be with my Angel.

Ashima was standing in the lobby of our home with me by her side. She was silent and had no reason to smile. The last few days she had tried to smile just for the sake of smiling, with no reason and motive behind it. She was trying to find answers to the questions she had in her mind. She knew she had to live alone for the rest of her life and standing alone was just a habit she would have to get used to. I would love to see her marry again and get settled. She had a long life to live, and this is not what she deserved. She was just twenty-four, an age when girls don't even marry, and she was forced to be called a widow. My soul was really in pain thinking about her future. Perhaps she would not think about someone else, but I hoped our parents would start thinking about it. Our life was perfect without the fact that we were nothing without each other, and for her, it was time to find herself without me.

She kept looking at the setting sun and asked me in her low voice, "Teddy, why did you leave me all alone?" I knew she spoke to herself, but I could hear her and wanted to answer her, knowing she could not listen to me. I came closer to her and said, looking into her eyes, "I am always next to you, my Angel, because you are my body and I am your soul. I took birth because of you and my existence is because of you."

I wanted to wipe away the tears which were rolling down her cheeks, but I could not. And then she questioned me again, "You are such a cheat, Teddy. You followed me cycling after school, why did you pedal so fast in our life?"

I had no answer to her question, but I replied after looking into her eyes for some time, "I wanted to ride with you always, but do not know what happened and why it happened."

She remained silent, staring at the sun which was merging into the sky and darkness was taking over. She looked at it unblinking and then said, "I loved sitting in the front seat of the car and looking outside through the windshield. Being your wife, it was my right to sit next to you, but now…" she paused and then continued, "But now, I will sit in the back seat throughout my life."

Her words were depressing, and I wanted to convey to her, that it was time for her to sit in the driver seat and drive her own life, without me and my memories.

Months back, Angel used to stand in this same balcony in the evening, waiting for my cab to come, and when I reached, she'd welcome me with her big smile. She was always ready with a big cup of tea, and we both used to enjoy it sip by sip from the same cup, chatting, hugging and smiling. We never realized how the evening time flew by with each other. And now, in contrast, every minute was tough to pass. While standing in the balcony, we both used to guess stuff about the people walking in the park downstairs – is the girl walking pregnant or just has a big tummy? Is the girl walking with that aunty her daughter or daughter-in-law? And many other guesses. Now we both could make assumptions alone, but we were not with each other to share our views and laugh. Chatting in the evening and standing on the balcony is such a simple thing in life, but you realize its importance when you die and can no longer do it. Ashima still comes every evening to the balcony with a cup of tea, but now not to drink it but to empty it in the flowerpot in which we had planted a hibiscus plant.

I still remember how excited she was when we brought this hibiscus plant. She wanted to fill our balcony with hibiscus flowers in all colours. I was smiling that day at her passion, and standing in pain today looking at the same hibiscus plant which was dying each day. Was she intentionally destroying our memory or was something else on her mind, I was not sure. But everyday she poured a cup of tea in its pot and would leave without even looking at it.

She moved inside the kitchen with dragging steps, as if someone was forcing her to walk. If I could read her correctly, it was her life which was getting wasted. She placed the cup in the sink and opened the tap to rinse her hands. She uses to scold me when I used to wash my hands and go without drying them, as her kitchen used to get wet. But I died without telling her that I did that intentionally, as I loved to get scolded by her. Her scolding gave me a feeling that yes, she had full control of me and she is mine.

She was about to go into her bedroom when her mobile rang. She picked it up and took a seat on the sofa, making herself comfortable. It was her mother.

"Hello Mama,"

"Hello Ashi beta, how are you?" her mom replied.

"Okay mummy, tell me, how are you all?" Ashima replied softly.

"We are also fine. I was thinking of having a family dinner tomorrow for a change," Mummy informed her.

"Leave it, Ma; there is no family without Kartik," Ashima concluded.

"Beta, I can understand your suffering, but it's life and we must not forget that no one can go against the almighty's wish." Mama explained and continued, "Maybe Kartik will also feel happy to see you smiling with your family."

Hearing her words, Ashima thought for a second and then changed her mind and replied, "Okay, I will tell Kartik's parents. When are you planning to have it?"

"Tomorrow evening. Should I send Rohit to pick you all?"

"No, it's okay, Papa can drive," Ashima replied.

"I am so happy that you've agreed, beta," Mama replied.

Ashima kept listening and then without speaking a word, she hung up and went into our bedroom.

18

Papa was driving, while Ashima sat on the back seat along with Mummy. Everyone was silent as the Noida-Greater Noida Expressway began. It was seven in the evening, and they were going for dinner to Ashima's parent's place. This was the same road on which I used to look at the stars with my Angel and the same place where I had met with the accident. There was nothing to talk; I was the chain joining them which had broken now. And now, each one was searching for their reason to live.

Ashima had started responding by a smile, but she was still in deep pain from which she was trying hard to come out. I was still not sure what was on her mind. That day I don't know how and when, but I reached the spot where I had died. I started looking everywhere and was surprised to find myself standing in the corner. I could hear every bit of sound by then, even the sound of the smallest creature crawling on the ground. I turned to check the leaves of the trees planted at the corner of the roads; they were moving with the wind of the passing cars. Their flickering sounds could be heard as if they were clapping and shouting, as real people do during bungee jumping.

I walked a few steps forward towards the busy road and started observing the speeding vehicles. Every vehicle looked blurry to me; I was not sure why and then I saw Papa driving his car at some distance. My eyes were stuck on it. It looked like time was under my control. I could observe his car driving in slow motion, while the nearby vehicles were moving fast, very fast. I was confused, but kept seeing our vehicle unblinking as it came closer. I remained standing in the corner as it approached towards me. I looked at Papa through the windshield as the car tried to cross me. I turned my face towards the moving direction of the car and my eyes coincided with Ashima's eyes, who was sitting in the back seat, facing towards me. I could see her dull face, lost in herself, unblinking, looking into my eyes as if trying to recognize me. I kept looking into her eyes to convey how much I loved her.

And then Papa applied the brakes suddenly, as Ashima shouted from behind, asking him to stop the car. I could see the friction with which the car tires stopped and dragged along the pebbles, marking the road with a screeching sound. Mummy jerked in shock, as she had been sitting relaxed. Ashima was pulling Papa's collar, asking him to stop the car. I saw the other cars halting suddenly to avoid a collision and making their way to the side.

I could not understand what had happened. Then the back door opened, and Ashima stepped out in a rush. She was staring straight at me. With a bulging stomach, nine months pregnant, she tried her best to run towards me, dropping her purse on the tar road. Papa also opened the door just after her and rushed behind her, shouting at her to stop, "Ashima, what happened? Stop… you will get hurt."

But she was not going to listen to anyone as she replied, "Papa, it's Kartik standing in that corner. I saw him! Kartik, I love you… I am coming… wait for me…"

I was not sure how that had happened, but yes, she could see me or feel me for that instance. I was astonished when she said that she could see me, but I knew the distance was huge. I smiled as she ran towards me, to welcome her and hug her.

"There is no one there, beta," Mummy shouted from behind her, but she ran towards me nonetheless. I kept smiling at her as she moved towards me and then she stopped just about five meters away. Few cars had also stopped at the side, to know what was happening.

With a brooding face, she looked at the point where I was standing and then towards Papa. She pointed her finger towards me, and with the husky voice, she said, "Kartik was standing here Papa, I saw him. He was smiling at me."

She paused and walked towards the point where I was standing. With a grave look, she showed him the spot, "He was standing here… he is alive Papa, I could see him…"

Papa came close to her and hugged her as she started crying, still showing the same spot with her finger, "He was there, I know he was there!"

Yes, I was standing there, but lost in time and space.

"I can understand your pain beta, but one who leaves this earth never comes back," Papa tried to console her.

Meanwhile, Mummy came to her side, "Kartik is gone, beta. It's just your love which is searching for him everywhere."

"No Mummy, he was there, standing right here. He wanted to hug me…"

Mummy placed her hand on her head and tried to calm her. I knew she was right, she had seen me, or she had felt me, but I don't understand how this had happened and why. Maybe it was the love between us which was trying to bring me back to her, but it was just an illusion which we both had felt.

"I have seen him. Kartik was standing there. He was looking at me, as if asking me why I was not reaching out to him," Ashima was murmuring, while Papa was trying to console her in his arms, taking her back to the car. As humans, we can only believe what we see, touch and feel. And Ashima could not touch me anymore.

Papa was trying to calm her and take her back to the car, but then she stopped, looked at Papa's face and then pushed to move away from him. Papa moved to a distance but looked around realizing it was the spot where the accident had taken place.

Papa went quiet and so did Ashima. Suddenly a silence took over. Ashima hugged Papa, one whom she had hated a lot till then. She went back to the car herself, turning back again and again to see if I was still standing there. I was still waiting for her to hug me, through in vain. I was all alone in the other world.

Ashima took her seat in the car and waited for Papa to drive to Greater Noida. She did not speak a word after that.

Within fifteen minutes, they reached Ashima's parents' place. Papa knocked at their door, and after the formal greetings, everyone sat down. A sense of discomfort was in the air. Priya

Bhabhi understood the situation and tried to start a conversation. She asked Ashima to come along and took her to the kitchen. "So how are you doing, Ashima?" she questioned while serving the dinner in bowls.

Ashima nodded.

"Will you help me to take the food to the dining table?" Priya Bhabhi tried to make her busy.

Ashima again nodded and picked one bowl and went to the dining room, followed by Priya Bhabhi. My Papa was equally silent; it was only my mummy who tried to bridge the gap.

"The food is smelling so good. Very nice Priya Betaji," Mummy picked up a bowl and commented with a smile.

"Thanks, Auntyji, it's Ashima's favourite. Rohit told me she loves Paneer Butter Masala, so I made it for her," Priya Bhabhi replied placing the salad at the center of the table.

Ashima smiled taking a seat next to her mother around the dining table.

"Uncleji, please join for dinner. Papa, please come," Rohit invited them to the dining table. Papa stood to place his spectacles on the side table and took a seat next to my mummy, who was seated in front of Ashima.

"Please start, Auntyji. Feel free," Priya Bhabhi said.

Ashima took a little rice and some daal.

"Take this paneer butter masala, it's especially for you, Ashima," Ashima's mom said and placed a spoonful on her plate. Ashima didn't respond and started having her dinner. Time to time she smiled, that too without any reason.

Ashima's papa was about to take some rice, when Rohit interrupted, "Papa, your sugar levels are very high. Please do not eat rice."

"Why? What happened? Are you not taking medicines?" Mummy questioned, taking a bite.

"He is, Auntyji, but the tension he is under is spiraling the sugar levels out of control," Priya Bhabhi answered.

"I try to keep calm and relax, but since Kartik has gone, I can't," Ashima's papa replied softly.

"We can understand. The same is with him. He stopped talking and is always lost in himself. I tell him he must leave everything to god now, but..." Mummy replied.

"He is tense about Ashima's future, and so are we. She is just twenty-four, and she has her whole life in front of her," Ashima's mom continued.

Ashima kept listening to everyone absentmindedly.

"We are worried about her as well," Mummy replied.

There was silence for a few minutes. Then Ashima's papa broke the silence saying in a low voice, "We must plan to make her marry again. Maybe we can find some good boy for her."

Papa stopped eating; his hands froze. Mummy went into thinking mode, chewing her food slowly.

Ashima's mom placed her hand on my Mummy's and asked, "Hope you agree with us. We understand she is your daughter now, but we as her parents, we can't sleep thinking about her every night."

Before Mummy or Papa could reply, Ashima stood from the chair and walked towards the kitchen without saying a word.

"Do you need something Ashima? Let me help you," Priya Bhabhi questioned. Everyone looked at Ashima and was expecting her to say something, but she remained quiet.

Mummy looked into the eyes of Ashima's mom and replied, "I am also a mother and can understand your concern. I've lost my son and know what the meaning of that is. I am smiling everyday, caring for everyone, because I know if I lose faith and strength, there is no one to take care of all three of us. We are getting old, and we won't be in a position to take care of Ashima and her baby," she paused, looked down and continued, "We agree with you."

As she completed her sentence, the sound of steel plates clanging could be heard from the kitchen. Hearing that, Priya Bhabhi stood up, "Ashima, what happened? Is everything fine?"

I followed her and found Ashima pulling out wheat flour from a container into the plate and trying to knead the dough. She was pouring water into the flour and was mixing it fast with her hands as if she was pouring her anger into it.

She was still silent, but her expressions and actions were sufficient to show what she was trying to convey. "What are you doing Ashima? Leave it! There is dough in the fridge, it's not required," Priya Bhabhi said trying to hold her hand. But she was not going to stop. Ashima pushed Priya Bhabhi's hand and continued mixing the dough. Her body and face were moving front and back, as she was kneading the dough.

"Rohit, please look at what Ashima is doing," Priya Bhabhi called out to Rohit.

Rohit and the others rushed towards the kitchen. Everyone was stunned into silence watching her, as she continued with rage on her face. After waiting for a minute, Rohit went to her and hugged her holding her face. He tried to stop her from the exertion.

"Stop sister. Please stop, I can understand your discomfort," Rohit tried to calm her down.

Ashima buried her face in his chest, while her tears started rolling. Then she pushed the plate of dough down with a bang and let out a cry. She broke down into sobs. She had come to her parents to relax, but left with more pain. The wheat flour was all over her face and hair as she cried calling my name.

"I am married to Kartik in this lifetime and can never think about anyone else," Ashima cried and continued pleading. "Leave me alone, please leave me alone. I will take care of our baby."

She slumped to the ground losing her strength to stand and continued, "Please leave me alone."

"We understand Ashima. Do not worry; you will never be forced to marry. I promise you."

No one knew what was in her mind, but yes, as her family, everyone was concerned. Everyone understood she loved me, but one cannot survive with memories alone. With time, memories fade away in the everyday fight for bread. This is the truth of life, and our parents could foresee that. Everyone had accepted that I was just a stop in her life, but not the destination. She had a long way to go and to live without a companion is never an easy task. What time had in its kitty will only be revealed in its own time, but we as humans can just plan that time to come up with better memories to cherish later.

19

That night, Ashima was thoughtful. Even just thinking about a second marriage was like a sin for her. She pulled her knees up to her chest and wrapped her arms around her shins. If she could just curl up into a wrapper and not face the realities of life. But she still had to live with herself, with the sad memories swirling around in her head. Her eyes were red and puffy as she had cried for a long time. She squeezed them shut to push more tears out. She let her head fall to her knees, and pulled her legs closer to herself, taking care of her baby.

After spending some more time in the same position, she opened the wooden box to read my last letter to my baby. My letters had been her reason to live since the last few days and today was the last one. But she knew she could read my letters again and again. My letters seemed like the light at the end of the tunnel, and she felt energetic after reading them. She opened the box in the silence of her breaths. Even the sound of her touch on the box could be heard in the room.

She picked up the last letter which was wrapped around a hard rectangular box. Ashima wanted to guess what it was, but she was in a hurry to read my letter. She tried to unfold the wrapper and found my picture in a wooden frame. She was surprised as she could not understand why my picture was wrapped with that letter. With excitement in her eyes, she opened the letter.

My dearest Baby,

How are you, my baby? I am sure you are great and why not? You are a child of parents who love you the most and love each other the most in this world. Sometimes I feel it's your mama and me who were Adam and Eve when this earth was formed, and we have been taking birth since then to spread love and get loved by each other.

Are you laughing at me? C'mon I am serious, baby

I could observe the smile on Ashima's face, as if some extra oxygen had got pumped into her lungs.

Today, you know, while I am writing this letter, I am happy as well as sad. Happy because I am interacting with you and I can see your Mama sleeping in front of me, and sad because my Papa, your grandfather is at our place and he is not interacting with me.

It's not that your mama and I are not trying to make things normal, but till now all our efforts have been wasted. I love Papa a lot, as you love me, and I am sure by the time you will be reading or hearing this letter, your grandfather would have forgiven me, and we'll both be playing with you.

Your grandfather has been angry with me for a long time, but with your mama, I'll bring him back into my life. Your mother is a full dose of multi-vitamins and fresh air. She is my energy and reason to live.

When I wake up in the morning, I am already fresh as your mother wakes me up with a kiss. During office hours I am never tired because she keeps sending me messages to make me smile. I never get bored travelling in office cabs, as I keep looking at your mother's pictures on my mobile. I never feel tired at home, as she is always there to energize me.

I always plan to write a letter for you, to tell you something different, but I land up talking about your mama, as she is the only one in my head, my heart, and my breath.

I am not sure how long is my life, but I pray to god every morning, that take me before you take my love, as she is strong to handle my memories, but I am just a piece of flesh without her. She is someone who knows how to handle life, and I am sure in my absence, she will make your life the best possible.

But why am I writing such a sad story, as I am sure I will be living long, till ninety-nine. So just happiness and smiles from now on.

Okay, so now, you'll be guessing why my picture is in this letter. Today I thought what I must put with this letter, and when I didn't find anything special, I packed my old school picture. I am sure your mama will love to look at this image, as she was the one standing in front of me at the studio and made me laugh to make this picture a perfect one.

You may gift this picture to your mama, or you may keep it wherever you like. But remember one valuable lesson in life:

'pictures are meant to tell you what you were so that you can always try to improve from your past.'

Bye for now.

Love you,
Your Teddy Papa

She picked up the photograph, and that was all it took for her dam of tears to burst. She clutched the solid wooden frame tight in her hand, and was able to see a reflection of her face in the thin sheet of glass that covered it. She looked past her own dreary eyes and stared upon her face, bringing back all memories within milliseconds. The happiest memories hurt the worst; they were the ones that cut her the deepest. She focused on my picture, which was glistening with the twinkle of the laughter that she had once loved. Now there were hardly any smiles. My picture reminded her of what she had lost. She clutched the frame tight, pressing it hard to her chest, wishing to feel my head resting upon it one last time.

She leaned back taking the support of the pillow, still crying. Then she looked surprised and confused. I came close to her to check her facial expression as she looked concerned. She moved her hand down, leaving my picture, to check her clothes. To her surprise, they were wet. Without wasting a moment, she screamed to call my Mummy. She tried to lay back on her back, trying to stop the fluid flow. She started feeling contractions stronger and more rhythmically. She decided to change her position to let the contractions subside, but they grew stronger and more regular. She knew the time had come for the baby to see the world.

It took all her strength to scream further to call Mummy, who was in deep sleep at two in the morning. Once a woman's water breaks, the baby is no longer surrounded by a protective fluid and could be at risk of developing an infection.

I rushed to check if Mummy had heard her, and thanks to god, she just pushed the door open as I turned.

"What happened, Betaji?" Mummy questioned rushing towards her.

"Water broke, I think," Ashima replied in pain.

Papa also came rushing, "Is everything fine?" he questioned.

"No, her water broke. Call an ambulance. She's going into labour," Mummy replied to Papa anxiously and rushed to collect some clean clothes and pads. Papa, understanding the situation, went outside the room to get his mobile.

Soon after, her labour started. With each contraction came a pain that dominated Ashima's entire being. Her stomach tightened, and she could hear herself scream.

Papa knocked on the door and informed Mummy as she came out, "No ambulance is available immediately. Can we wait for an hour?"

"No, I don't think we should wait, she already had a complication. Let me call Rashmi," Mummy replied and closed the room.

Mummy helped Ashima to place the pad and asked her to relax as she was in great pain and took her mobile to call Rashmi.

"Rashmi Beta, Ashima's water is leaking, and I think labour has started."

Mummy listened to what Rashmi explained to her and then opened the door after hanging up.

"*Sunte ho,* Rashmi is saying we must take her immediately to Appollo Hospital, without wasting time. She says not to wait for the ambulance. What to do? Rashmi is also rushing to the hospital," Mummy was in tension, and the house was echoing with Ashima's screams, as the pain started becoming unbearable for her.

The tension on Papa's face was quite visible, as he was trying to figure out what to do. And then he did something for what he will be my hero. He rushed inside my bedroom, still in his pyjamas and a long pink shirt, and after monitoring Ashima for a second, he lifted her in his arms.

"Open the door!" he told my mother, and without wasting a single second, Mummy picked up the home and car keys and rushed to open the main door. With controlled feet, Papa carried Ashima in his arms, down the stairs, while Mummy rushed to lock the door.

Ashima was struggling in pain and looked serious as her water was dripping throughout. Papa carried her like his baby, asking her to keep calm in between. Mummy took faster steps and reached downstairs before Papa, and opened the door of the car for him. Ashima kept holding his shoulders tight as he arrived at the car. Carefully, Papa made her lie comfortably in the back seat. Mummy squeezed in and started cleaning Ashima's forehead with a clean napkin she was carrying, placing her head on her lap.

"Just relax, Betaji, we'll reach the hospital soon," Mummy consoled Ashima, while Papa started to drive.

It was the biggest day of our life. Our baby was coming into the world. How unlucky was I, who could not welcome him. I was cursing myself for not being with my Angel at the time she needed me the most.

Within no time, Papa drove to the hospital and took his car directly to the entrance of the emergency ward. Rashmi and Sanjeev were already waiting at the gate. Sanjeev was in his night suit. Papa opened the door and the ward boy helped to bring Ashima out of the car and put her on a stretcher. They hurried through the double doors; the wheels of the stretcher and pounding footsteps was all I could hear.

"Uncle, don't worry. Please go with the nurse, she will explain to you the formalities to be done," Sanjeev explained, while Rashmi started observing Ashima's heartbeat on her way to the labour room. Dr Sangeeta also joined in. Within no time, Ashima was taken to the labour room.

"I entered along with them and reached the door, brown and dull like all the others. I could already see the doctors and nurses in green gowns inside.

"Okay Ashima, so here we are, for the day we've all been waiting for," Rashmi smiled kindly and opened the drawer on her side. Doctors and nurses surrounded her bed, attaching IVs, heart monitors and other things to her. I kept my eyes on my Angel, who was sweating with pain.

Dr Sangeeta asked the nurse to pull the ultrasound machine and soon she started examining Ashima, placing the probe on her belly. Ashima was screaming as if every bone of her body was breaking into a thousand pieces.

"We must operate at once. The placenta is lying near the cervix, and it may block the baby's exit route through the vagina," Dr Sangeeta said watching the ultrasound monitor.

"Get the operation formalities completed by the family," Dr Sangeeta suggested.

Hearing her, Rashmi rushed outside where Sanjeev was waiting with my parents. "Sanjeev, get the operation formalities completed; we are starting her operation."

"Is everything fine?" Mummy asked Rashmi.

"Nothing to worry aunty, all good doctors are here for her," Rashmi tried to calm her. As Sanjeev took Papa to complete the formalities, Rashmi rushed back inside.

By the time Rashmi entered, Ashima was given local anesthesia. I stood next to her in tension, with folded hands in prayers.

Dr Sangeeta picked up the scalpel and made a horizontal cut under my Angel's belly.

20

Three days after Ashima got operated upon, I was standing in the balcony, all alone, waiting for my Angel to arrive from the hospital. The sun sank lower in the sky, letting the light of the day drain away, giving way to the darkness of the night. I could hear crickets chirping and the buzz of mosquitoes. I turned to check the street lights which were switched on, and the first star started blinking in the night sky. The garden in the front was blooming with yellow and purple flowers, whose smell I could only imagine. But yes, they seemed to be welcoming my Angel and our baby.

I was not sure why I was not with her and waiting in the balcony, but waiting was the only world left with me. After some time I saw Rohit's car coming towards our home. A smile took over my face as I was about to welcome my Angel and our baby. I wanted to hug them both and say how much I loved them. As the car stopped, Rohit stepped out and went to open the door of the back seat where Ashima was sitting along with Mummy. Ashima was dressed in a pink salwar suit, holding our baby wrapped in a white and pink baby wrapping towel. She then stepped out carefully. From the balcony, I could see our baby wearing a soft pink cap, moving his head slowly. His soft pink hands were visible from there. Ashima placed her right hand behind the baby's head to give support as she walked towards the main door of our home.

Rohit picked up their bags filled with baby stuff and Ashima's clothes, followed by Mummy and Papa. As Ashima reached the door, she stopped and turned her face up to look at the balcony, as if she knew I was standing there waiting for her. After staying for a few seconds, she went inside towards the stairs.

"Hold the baby carefully," Mummy guided Ashima as they went up the stairs. Ashima nodded, taking small steps. She was holding the baby tight as if he was everything for her now, and by looking into her eyes, it was clear she was talking to me in her mind.

Papa opened the lock of the main door and entered to switch on the lights, while Ashima stopped at the door, lost in her thoughts. She stood there with a vacant face when Rohit asked her to move inside.

"Kartik wanted to welcome his baby with his letters," Ashima replied softly.

"Letters?" Rohit questioned

"He was writing letters to our baby, which he wanted to gift me on this day." A drop of tear rolled down her cheek as she said this.

"He is not with us today, but I want him to be with me forever."

She paused, brought the baby in front of her so that she could look at the face of a baby and continued, "Today, I want to give his son a name; a name which I gave to him; a name which we loved; a name hearing which he smiled." She again paused, continued looking at our baby and then kissed him on his forehead.

"Your name will be the name of the most beautiful person who lived on this earth," she again paused and then concluded, "Teddy." And Ashima then burst into tears, hugging our baby.

Our baby looked at her with his big black eyes. His tiny hands wrapped up in a soft little blanket wanted to wipe away her tears. His legs kicked in a tiny jagged motion, looking for that resistance they were used to I guess, but finding none. And then he smiled, softly, just lifting his lower lips.

Mummy immediately hugged her with tears in her eyes, while Rohit wiped her tears with his fingers. Ashima then stepped inside and walked to our bedroom. The bed was neatly made and adjusted with the perfect place for the baby to sleep. Ashima placed the baby at the center of the bed and set pillows on the sides. Our little Teddy was there with his gorgeous smile.

Ashima stood up slowly. She went in front of the mirror and looked at the smiley sticker and began to smile again. She waited for sometime and watched herself in the new role of a mother, and as she turned, she saw something placed on a desk. In front of my wooden framed picture. Next to the wooden box of letters.

It was a white coloured envelope addressed to '*My Dearest Wife.*'

A nostalgic wave rushed through her mind as she picked it up and found written below, '*Your Teddy*'.

An envelope was for her this time, and not the baby. 'How could Teddy write me a letter?' must be a question which came to her mind. She picked up the envelope and sat down on the chair. With frozen hands and a racing heartbeat, she opened the envelope. There was a letter inside. Before reading, she again turned the envelope to check the post office seal to know from where that letter had come. It said Noida.

With shaking hands, she opened the letter, which was written with a black gel pen. I stood behind her to have a look and found it was my handwriting. Before starting to read, she looked at the letter and caressed at it as if I was sitting in front of her. With wet eyes and love for my memories, she started reading the letter:

My Dearest Wife,

I write this letter with much love and fondness for you, who is my one and only adorable wife. I hope that your day be enlightened with the brightest sun forever and may its rays tell you that I am there at all times for you. My loving wife Ashima, you raise my soul every time I think of you. You are my sunrise and my shining star!

I remember how nervous and excited I was when I planned exactly how I would ask you to marry me. How that ice cream melted in our hands, how I could hardly wait to see your delight and joy when I asked you to be my wife. You were the most beautiful girl in the world to me. I just knew that I had to have you for myself. Thank you for accepting me and not trying to change me. I was honored to be your husband. You are indeed a gift from god. My life was so much better because you were there with me.

Ashima sobbed as she started reading the letter. She wiped her tears which were about to fall on the letter and continued,

Nothing can beat the feeling I had when we were together. Knowing you were there with me and that we could overcome anything was a great feeling. You made me feel so much better when you were near. I wanted to feel that forever, even being a soul.

You'll be wondering and will be astonished at how I am writing this letter to you when I am no longer alive. I cannot answer that, but remember, the almighty is always there to help his children and with his grace, I could connect with you again.

My body got burnt to ashes but my soul is with you, and my love is with you as our baby.

Ashima stopped and started looking around as if she could feel me near her. Her sad eyes began searching for me all over. And then she again concentrated on reading,

Never search for me, as I am always within you. I am in the breath you take; I am in every move you make; I am in your eyes; I am in your smile.

Promise me something, my Angel, you will never tell anyone about my letters to you. Every month, you will be getting a letter from me, but only till you can keep it a secret. You are the most precious gift I've had in my life, and it's your responsibility to take care of my gift. Till I was alive, I loved watching you smiling and laughing. Please, I beg you, I want to keep watching you do the same.

You know how much I loved your nails painted with nail paint. It hurts me seeing your bare nails now. You were my dream girl, and you are still my dream girl, no matter if I am alive or not.

I love you so much; more than words can express. You drove me to be a better person for myself and you. Thank you for being the most fantastic woman in the world. But since the day I died, you have stopped taking care of yourself; it is hurting me a lot. I am in the world from where I can see you firmly, but cannot bring back a smile on your face. Promise me, you will be as amazing as ever and will give me reasons to smile as a soul.

Being away from you, I am only left with your memories with me. Please do not let them fade away with your changed attitude. Your positivity was my strength, and it is even today. Wipe off your negative thoughts to give me the power again.

Remember my words – you are never alone on this earth. If you are alive, you have a purpose to live, and you need to keep searching for the key to happiness. Remember, we live once, but we die multiple times if your loved ones are not happy. Please save me from dying again.

I could see my Angel nodding while reading the letter. Her sobbing sound was enough to disturb our sleeping baby.

Our baby was our dream and today he is in your arms. I am so proud of you. Wish I would have been with you, but still, I am with you. You need to do me a favour, and I do not want to hear no for it. Go for a professional photoshoot for our baby, and you must be a part of it. You might not be able to see me, but I will be present in every frame.

You are the only one whom I loved when alive and you are the only one whom I still loved when I died. You are the most beautiful truth I had; you are the most beautiful past I lived; and you are the most attractive future I would feel.

Time will be tough for you as you move ahead; never lose hope and faith in god. Time gives pain, but it also heals the wounds it gives. Whenever you need me, I'll always be by your side in some or the other way; you just need to find me.

One last time, I would like to convey, I feel the pain when you get hurt, and no medicine works on the soul.

My love, my Angel, promise me you will live your life to the best, as I being a soul can understand the importance of life. I want you to smile; I want you to laugh; I want you to live your dreams; I want you to fulfill my thoughts; I want all that because I am still your husband and friend who loved you and loves you to the core of my heart and soul.

It's time to let go of the life we planned, and to accept the one waiting for you.

Whatever you do in your life, trust me, I am always here with you.

Love you forever, my dearest wife.

Yours and only yours,
Teddy

Ashima remained seated on the chair, eyes closed. Her chest heaved with a quiet sob, and tears welled up behind her eyelids, slipping down her cheeks without resistance. Another sob wracked her, followed by a thin wail. She opened her eyes and wept with her shoulders heaving.

I went down on my knees in front of her, head down and cupped my palms to catch the precious tear drops. I could see the drop, sprinkling towards my hands, and pierced my palm to hit the floor.

I remained seated observing her. She was still crying holding the letter in her hand. And it seemed she had decided something. She took a deep breath in one go. Tightened her collarbone and straightened her backbone, to wipe away her tears before they even tried to make the path down her eyes. She started rubbing them with her hands, one after the other, until they stopped.

Ashima then stood up from her chair and went to the mirror and started looking at herself in confidence. She looked at the smiling sticker on it and then turned to check our baby. With a pause, she started looking herself again and then picked up the comb and started combing her hair. I stood next to her and smiled. She was coming back to life.

"It's your beautiful hair, which entangled me between life and death."

She then pulled open the drawer which she had not opened since my death, containing all her fancy wear and pulled out a pink coloured hairband. I still remember that was the prettiest hairband she had. I had bought it for her from Nanital.

"It's your pink hairband that makes you more beautiful, and troubles my eyes as they cannot blink further."

She then pulled her hair tight into a bun on the top of her head, exposing her long beautiful neck. As she bent to put her comb back, I could observe the mole on her neck, which was one of the reasons for my heart to beat.

"It's the mole behind your neck, which took away my heart whenever I kissed it."

Ashima then turned to open the door of her room wide open. She then walked straight to the balcony and after looking at the stars for a few minutes, pulled her hand with two fingers to select.

"Teddy, which finger would you select?" she questioned looking at the sky.

I moved with slow steps towards her and replied, "I select your index finger, my Angel."

After looking at the sky for a few more minutes, she selected both her fingers with her left hand and replied, "Today, both fingers questioned if I must start living again for you, for our baby and me." She paused and then continued, "And the reply is yes, I want to live. I want to live for your love; I want to live for your memories; I want to live to keep you alive; I want to live to love you more; I want to live for our baby."

This time she didn't cry, but smiled. Smiled as if she had found me back; smiled as if she had found a reason to live. She picked up the can filled with water and poured into the hibiscus pot, giving it a new life.

21

One-and-a-half years later

Our baby was one year six months old now. He had started walking and ran to every corner of the house in Dehradun. Yes, Ashima had shifted with my parents to Dehradun and had begun teaching in the same school from where we had passed out.

Teddy had grown to a very active, cute and loving child. He never troubled his mother, Dada or Dadi. I felt happy to see Papa playing with Teddy and teaching him the same values which he had once taught me. But now, he never talked about engineering. Mummy spent most of her time with Teddy, as she felt I was back in him.

Ashima was partially out of her trauma and started living her life. She still slept with the lights switched on and avoided talking to Papa. But yes, her nails were painted now.

Sanjeev and Rashmi got married two months back. Rashmi is now a really good friend of Ashima, and they both talk every single day, without fail. They both can gossip for hours.

I am still with my Angel all the time and wondering why I am still waiting on this earth and what is my purpose?

Every first day of the month, Ashima was still receiving the letters signed by me, and she excitedly waited for them. Every note brought a message of motivation to her to live and do what best she could do to make her and Teddy's life great. She religiously followed whatever was asked in the letter. She had agreed to move to Dehradun; she had agreed to smile again; she had agreed to start working; and she had agreed to get married again.

I am thankful to the person who was writing those letters in my name because that had helped her come out of her pain. She might know it's not me who was writing the letters, but she wanted to continue to live in that illusion of me being with her.

✦

I was standing with Ashima, my wife, in our bedroom. She was all set to leave for the banquet hall, holding a bouquet of red roses in her hand. She was dressed in a red lehenga with golden work and a dupatta over her head. She was looking as beautiful as ever. Her hands adorned with red and gold bangles were creating a magical effect on her soft white hands.

I loved her lips and complimented her. Today when they are glowing with wine coloured lipstick, I could not take my eyes away from them. Ashima sat in front of the dressing mirror.

Standing behind her, I looked at her with a smile on my face.

Her deep thinking eyes were looking gorgeous with perfectly lined eyeliner. With the fine make-up and hair-do, looked ravishing.

The sound of guests laughing and chatting outside our room was not distracting me that day. I got was in her beauty which I'd miss forever in a few hours. But I am happy today.

"Kartik, I am sorry for leaving you today. You know that I will miss you forever. I know you are hoping that I'd stay, but it's just impossible. We started our love story when we were children, and today, I need to move on, and that too for your love. You were always with me when I needed you, and today, when I am taking a new path in my life, I will not say that I will miss you, because we only miss someone whom we forget. You are a part of my soul, my breath, and my life and I will always love you, until my last breath."

I could feel her pain. I could see tears rolling down her cheeks, but that day I could not stop her from crying, because I was happy. It was her wedding day. She kept looking at the mirror, while I stood behind her, watching her.

I wanted to shout, but no one wanted to hear my voice. I wanted to come back, but it was too late. I wanted to hug her again, but she was no longer mine. Because it was her wedding day – my wife's wedding.

She stood holding her lehenga and turned towards me. She looked beautiful as never before and I wanted to hold her and never let her go. But instead, I took two steps back and went to the balcony to let my soul cry.

Rashmi knocked on the door and entered laughing, "Oh! Gorgeous lady, let's go to the mandap. Mr Anurag is waiting eagerly."

Ashima was getting married to Anurag, a common friend of Rashmi and Sanjeev. He was also a doctor. Ashima nodded with a smile and went to Teddy who was sleeping on the bed.

"Teddy, your Mama will be back soon."

"Do not worry about our hero; I will take care of him," Rashmi replied smiling and hugging Ashima.

"Ladies, we must go down now," Sanjeev interrupted knocking at the door and continued, "If you get late, Anurag will leave for another surgery and then it would be tough to catch him." They all laughed.

Ashima strolled towards the mandap when Mummy joined her with a smile filled with love and blessings.

"You are the most beautiful daughter on this earth; we are blessed to have you with us."

Papa stood by Ashima's father's side, looking older and less energetic that day.

"Kartik and Ashima got married on 30 June and today again is the same date. What a coincidence!" Ashima's father told my Papa. Hearing him, Papa came back to life and started feeling energetic.

"Excuse me. I will be back," Papa replied and started walking cleaning his specs.

As Ashima took her steps towards the mandap to get married again, I started losing energy in my soul. I came down among all the guests, but the scene in front of me was getting faded. I could hear many sounds together, but nothing was clear. I started looking around, wondering what was happening to me, but did not get a single clue. I saw Papa rushing towards the house, crossing the mob of guest gathering for the ritual of garland exchange. His old feet suddenly had a new surge of energy, as if he was losing time. He placed his specs back and rushed past the guests.

I found his behaviour strange and started following him. The picture in front was getting faded, and I could hardly recognize the people I was crossing. But I kept following Papa.

Papa reached the main door of our house and entered without speaking a word to anyone. I found that my hands remained by my side and I could not raise them again. I looked for Papa who had now reached his bedroom and was searching for something in the drawer.

I was not sure what he was searching for, but his expression showed he was worried. He then smiled as he found a pen. He pulled his chair and took out a piece of paper from the white paper bundle placed on his desk. I could not understand what he was doing, but then Mummy entered.

"Writing a letter to Ashima?" she asked softly on entering the door.

"Yes, just remembered today is the thirtieth and if I'll not post it today, it will not reach her on time," Papa replied after seeing her.

Mummy entered and pulled up a chair next to him.

"I understood you had missed the letter this month because of the wedding preparations, when I saw your worried face."

I could hear them speaking, but now the sound was echoing, as if some old cassette was playing. I was happy to find they both still understood their wordless expressions.

"She is starting a new life. I am not sure what I must write as Kartik today," Papa replied placing the pen back on the paper.

Mummy placed her hand on his shoulder and replied, "You are the one who was Kartik's mentor; you taught him writing holding his hands; you taught him how to cycle; you taught him the values of life; you made him alive after death."

She paused and then continued, "You can write the letter because you know exactly what Kartik would have thought at this moment. See, that's why our son used to call me every single day and used to tell me every little thing about Ashima and himself. Now, his voice has become words, which has helped Ashima to start her new life."

She wiped her tears, and Papa picked up his pen again. I could not see them clearly, their faces were fading off, but I was thankful to my parents who had helped in brining Ashima back to life. Papa was always my hero, and he had proved it yet again.

"We lost our son, but we got a daughter for life. She may not speak to me and continue to believe me to be responsible for Kartik's death, but for me, she is my daughter and she has all the rights to show her grievances. And I respect her for that."

After a pause, he placed the pen back and burst out crying. He had been holding his tears back for years, and today he let them out. His emotions came out with a shiver, as his body shook. As he sobbed aloud, his lower lip went wet. He wept with all his heart and soul.

Mummy placed her hand on his hair and hugged him, without asking him to stop crying.

"I lost my son, my Kartik, and today, I am losing my daughter," he said wiping his eyes.

"No, we are not losing her, we are bringing Kartik back in Anurag."

The positive reply from Mummy helped him gather himself.

"Auntyji, you are sitting here! Their garland exchange ritual has started," one of Ashima's cousins informed from the door.

"Oh! Yes, I am coming," Mummy replied excitedly, and asked Papa, "Let's go, it's a big day for our daughter. You may complete the letter after this ritual."

Papa stood and went along with Mummy.

I was losing all my strength. My feet stopped moving, but I wanted to be with my Angel as she was about to start her new life. I tried to drag myself in the faded view. I looked all around and felt as if snow had covered the surroundings. Everything around me was turning white. I applied all my strength to drag myself, but found myself entering into a hallucination.

As I strolled along, I saw Ashima at some distance as a young schoolgirl, wearing red ribbons in her hair and cycling. I looked at her and smiled as she turned toward me and shouted, "Teddy, come fast, catch me." I felt as if she was calling me from very far. I applied more strength to reach her, but before I could, she called me from another side.

"Teddy, see I have bought an ice cream pack for you. Come to me. We will have an ice cream wedding again." She showed me a pack of ice cream, smiling, and started moving away. I raised my hand to grab her, but could not. I was not able to understand what was happening to me, but I followed her.

As I dragged myself into the white atmosphere, I saw Ashima standing at some distance with a big tummy with both her hands placed on her stomach, wearing a white evening gown.

"Teddy, see our baby is kicking a lot. I could not stop laughing. Touch me here, you will also feel his presence." I tried raising my hands to touch her, but she vanished in the white light. Was my time nearing to leave her forever? No, god. Please help. I wanted to be with my Angel forever and ever.

Finally I felt I had reached near the mandap where the garland exchange ritual was going on. I could see my Angel dressed as a bride at some distance. I turned to check Mummy smiling at her. Papa was laughing carrying my son. Everyone was smiling and getting faded at the same time. I understood it was not them who were fading away, but my memories which were fading away.

I turned as Ashima called me from behind, dressed as a bride, "Teddy, tighten my earring, it's loose." I tried raising my hand, but failed and she again vanished.

I smiled and shouted, "Angel, I love you." But she could not listen to me; my voice came back as an echo. I tried to walk closer to her.

"Kartik, my Teddy." I heard Ashima from the side. I turned to check her. She was standing in front, submerged in the white light like a snow princess.

"I love you, Teddy," she replied and presented me with two fingers. "Teddy, pick one of them."

I looked at her with a smile. I was feeling thirsty as if I had not drunk water for years. I could feel the cracking of my lips as I replied with my full strength, "Not now Angel, I am feeling lost in this white light."

She continued smiling at me and showed me her fingers to pick. I tried to keep looking at her, but my eyes were getting closed as if I was going into a coma.

"Pick a finger Kartik, my Teddy," Ashima again shouted.

I smiled and gathered all my strength for one last time and jumped to grab her fingers, shouting, "I love you, my dearest wife."

I fell to the ground and saw white light enveloping me. I tried to get up, but got buried in the light. My eyelids were closing with the pressure, though I wanted to open them.

I lost all hope and strength to get up again, and before the final closing of my eyes, I saw from very far that my Angel, my Ashima had placed the garland around Anurag's neck, and smiling faces were praising and blessing the couple.

I realized the meaning of life and death. I understood, that to begin something, many things need to end. I closed my eyes peacefully, to finish the old, and open my heart to a new beginning.

If I did anything perfect in my life, it was when I gave my heart and soul to you, my dearest wife. Maybe in memories, but I am always here with you.

Yours,
Teddy

By the same author

MY MUTE GIRLFRIEND

Rohan is a telecom professional posted in Meerut and misses his girlfriend from college days, who had stopped interacting with him, without giving any reason. Although she had always stood by his side and her eyes reflected immense love, but she remained his mute girlfriend.

    The book opens with an SMS from Vaidehi to Rohan, after five long years. But before he could reply, his mobile gets damaged and he wanders in his memories to narrate a story.

    My Mute Girlfriend is a true romance story of how Rohan unravels the answers to why Vaidehi was mute for so long, and how their life is about to change. But little do they know that the worst is yet to come.

You can now reach out to your favourite author directly.
Email him on himanshurai80@rediffmail.com
or
WhatsApp him on 8810329026